Every Time, Any Place

Every Time, Any Place

L.D. Skinner

VANTAGE PRESS
New York

This is a work of fiction. Any similarity between the names and characters in this book and any real persons, living or dead, is purely coincidental.

Cover design by Susan Thomas

FIRST EDITION

Published by Vantage Press, Inc.
419 Park Ave. South, New York, NY 10016

Manufactured in the United States of America
ISBN: 978-0-533-15810-2

Library of Congress Catalog Card No: 2007903384

0 9 8 7 6 5 4 3 2 1

To my husband, John,
and my sons, Brian and Patrick, for without their
support and belief,
this book would have never come to pass

Every Time, Any Place

Prologue

Time: Summer 2005.

Place: Edinburgh, Scotland—The picnic area of the First Presbyterian Church.

The sound of children's laughter was the first thing Lysette Duncan became aware of as she opened her eyes from a daze. She shook her head slightly and pressed her fingertips against her temple to try and clear it. The sun was very bright as she focused her vision in the direction of the sound and shielded the harsh rays by placing her hand on her foreheads just above her eyebrows.

The children were scrambling around on some large, rather odd-looking objects, the likes of which she had never seen before. She concluded then that it must be a play area of some type, for all the fun they seemed to be having.

She proceeded to glance around and spotted several adults nearby. Some were milling about in groups conversing and laughing, while others were sitting as small wooden tables eating. There was a long table set up in the middle of it all with enormous amounts of food spread out over it. An appetizing aroma filled the air and reached her nostrils. Her stomach grumbled at the smell as she realized she must not have eaten yet.

Where was this place? she thought to herself. She did

not recognize it, and for that matter, how did she come to be here? She searched her mind for answers and found to her dismay she could not recall. The people were all dressed in an unusual manner. They were out in public for goodness sake, scantily dressed in fabrics such as undergarments. They were so bright and colorful. It was positively indecent to be outside in so few clothes. *What must these people be thinking?*

She looked farther off in the distance and spied what resembled a church, but a little different, and not as grand as what she was used to. A momentary feeling of relief washed over her at the sight. Maybe she could ask for help there. Her mind was filled with hazy confusion. She started to walk in that direction, but suddenly jumped back in startled fright. *What was that?* her mind screamed. Something whizzed by so fast; she hardly had enough time to make out what is was. She was able to notice, though, that there appeared to be people inside. It must be a conveyance of some sort, but how could this be? It had no horses pulling it. *How was it able to move?*

This must be a nightmare, some freakish dream her subconscious was making up while she was sleeping. She folded her arms close around her chest and hugged herself tightly. No! She was definitely awake. She stood there in awe, her mind working to try and make some sense of this situation. To an onlooker, she might appear to be contemplating taking her own life, hovering on the edge of the road, staggering slightly, just before stepping out into the traffic.

Her attention was diverted from her reverie, as she heard an urgent shout. Lysette turned toward the sound and saw an attractive young woman heading her way. She appeared to be beckoning to her, which confused Lysette even more. The woman seemed friendly enough, but Lysette was wary of a perfect stranger who was so oddly dressed. She began to back up a little.

"Hello there," the woman called out to her. "May I help you with something? You seem a little lost."

Lysette stood there, still silent, just observing the woman coming nearer.

"We're having a church picnic this afternoon, as you can see," the stranger went on to explain when Lysette seemed reluctant to answer her hail. "And I was not aware the Reverend had also scheduled a wedding to take place. He did not mention it in his sermon this morning, which is odd, since he always mentions when he is to perform a member's marriage. I don't recognize you, though. Are you new to our church? Would you like me to get the Reverend for you?"

Lysette frowned oddly and wondered why this woman was speaking to her of her wedding. That is, until she glanced down at herself, and saw that she was wearing the most exquisite wedding gown she had ever laid eyes on. A look of pure shock flashed across her features and she felt like she was going to faint.

The woman saw Lysette falter and hurried her step a little faster to reach her.

"Are you all right?" she asked with genuine concern.

Lysette was speechless.

"Who are you? What is your name?" the woman then uttered with emphasis, hoping this mysterious troubled soul could provide her with an answer.

Lysette was about to do just that when it suddenly dawned on her that she could not answer, for she had no earthly idea *who* she was.

1

Summer, 1705

Castle Campbell—Edinburgh, Scotland

THE ELEVENTH EARL OF CAMDEN, Colwyn Campbell, stood anxiously by the chapel altar as he waited nervously for the arrival of his lovely bride-to-be. He looked extraordinarily handsome in his white-ruffled silk shirt, dress kilt, black velvet jacket and clan-crested tam. His stylishly long, golden brown hair, which usually hung in thick waves, curled in riotous tendrils from perspiration around his face. If his intended lady fair looked upon him now, she would have thought he resembled a precocious child.

Never in Colwyn's wildest dreams had he ever imagined he could want this day to happen so much. That it was here was testimony both to good fortune and the privilege of birth.

The signal was given for the bagpiper to begin his tune. But suddenly there was heard a disturbance in the entryway. All eyes turned toward the commotion to see Amy Tuttle, Lysette's trusted friend and lady's maid, standing there, looking quite agitated. With her hand she silently and almost frantically beckoned Colwyn to her side. Naturally curious, every guest turned in her direction, wondering what could be causing the delay.

With evident concern and a puzzled look on his handsome face, Colwyn signaled for the bagpiper to cease his music then hurried to Amy's side. She drew him back and away from the seated guest's view so as not to alarm them.

"Oh, milord, I'm afraid we have a big problem!" she exclaimed in a breathless whisper. "When I went to fetch milady from the gardens, out back, I could find nary a trace of her!"

"What!" Colwyn nearly shouted his first response to the news but realized his blunder.

His next words were a harsh whisper, as he had no desire for others to overhear their conversation. "Amy, surely you're overreacting and causing a problem that does not exist! She must still be out there and just didn't hear you calling, that's all. And what, pray tell, was she doing out there anyway?" he asked as an afterthought. "Supposedly she was to be waiting upstairs for the signal."

"Lysette told me she was feeling a bit nervous and wanted to go out for a breath of fresh air. She said she wanted to be alone for a while to reflect on how fast her life was changing. I told her it was perfectly natural for her to feel a little jittery right a-fore she spoke her nuptials and all. Especially since she had only known her bridegroom for three days!" Amy emphasized.

"I was supposed to fetch her when it was time for the ceremony to begin, but I can't find her anywhere. I called and called her name but she didn't answer me.

"Ah!" Amy gasped as a horrible thought entered her mind. Now somewhat agitated and alarmed she spoke aloud her worst fears to Colwyn, "You don't suppose somebody spirited off with her, do you—maybe some of your enemies wanting, perhaps, to get their hands on some easy ransom?" Amy wailed and wrung her hands in distress and started to carry on something awful. "Oh, Lordy! I will never forgive myself if anything has happened to her!"

"Now, calm yourself, Amy," Colwyn said as he tried to reassure her while struggling to keep a cool head himself. "I doubt my enemies would be so bold as to try and cause harm today with the castle so heavily guarded.

"Let's go look again, Amy. I am sure we will find her. But we must hurry before the guests start to become restless or get suspicious."

The two hurried back out to the castle gardens, calling Lysette's name, softly at first, then their calls became louder and more frantic when they received no response.

Colwyn turned to confront Amy and told her, "Go back upstairs and check her room to see if for some reason she went back there."

"I already thought of that, Milord. I checked before I came back downstairs to report to you," Amy explained. "There just wasn't any sign of her there, either." Her body slumped in weary defeat.

"I can't be telling her father ov-this. It'd kill 'im," Amy said, her accent becoming more pronounced due to the fact she was so scared and anxious.

Colwyn was not yet ready to give up. In order to stop his thoughts from straying into a dark, despair-filled abyss, he knew he had to keep busy.

Once again, the two of them searched the gardens. In fact, they were sure they had looked into every square inch of the bloody area quite thoroughly. Still, they found no sign that she had even been there in the garden.

That is the most disturbing part of it all, Colwyn surmised to himself.

Amy was so worried she was near to fainting by this

time, and Colwyn had begun to lose a bit of his cool. "Now, Amy," his tone had become quite irritable, "you must tell me everything that transpired upstairs. What exactly did she say? How was she feeling? Speak up, woman, for we don't have all day!" he snapped. Colwyn had lost all his patience and with it, his sensitivity to other's feelings.

When he had shouted at her, Amy had become alarmed and began to cry and sob pitifully. Realizing his angry tone had frightened her and had only made matters worse, Colwyn took a deep breath and changed his tone so that became soothing and persuasive. In this new approach he now hoped to get the full story from her.

"It's all right, Amy," his voice soothed as he wrapped his arms loosely about her shoulders in an effort to calm her ruffled feathers. "I apologize for my brusqueness. Please forgive me! Now, could you tell me all that transpired as you know it since the beginning of this evening?"

"Well, let me see. . . ." Amy began in her thick Irish brogue, her voice still unsure and faltering breathlessly from her recent crying bout. "We was upstairs putting the finishing touches to her hair, when Miss said she was feeling a wee bit jumpy. As I told you a-fore, I explained to her it was perfectly natural for her to be a feeling at-a-way. She pleaded for a little air and solitude; said she'd been a-wanting to visit the gardens anyway since she had only glimpsed them shortly after we arrived here. At the time, she had commented on how lovely and well kept they were. So, when we were upstairs, just a short time ago, she told me she was going out to the garden to think on a few things and pray for a little wisdom and guidance before she embarked on her new life. When she left the room, she assured me she was fine, just wanted to be alone for a while. She even instructed me to be sure and fetch her when it was time. And you know the rest," Amy concluded.

"There's nothing more that you may have forgotten—something that in your frightened state over her disappearance you may have neglected to speak of perhaps?" Colwyn asked. He was puzzled that Amy had told him nothing really useful and that added even more confusion to the heart-wrenching mystery of his missing bride.

He pursued his questioning, hoping for at least a small clue. "She didn't say anything else? Maybe something that you don't feel comfortable telling me? Something you forgot, perhaps in your frightened state over her disappearance? Nothing unusual or out of the ordinary?"

"No, nothing!" Amy emphatically stated.

"I've told you everything I can remember," she insisted. "You know I wouldn't hold anything back!" Amy was very worried and distressed because he acted as if he didn't believe her and didn't bother hiding her feelings both in her facial expressions and actions.

"Yes, I know, Amy, and I'm genuinely sorry I accused you of something like that. It's just that I'm extremely worried. It may be hard for you to believe, but I really am in love with her," Colwyn confessed.

"I believe you milord," Amy assured him. "The minute I saw you looking at my Lysette for the first time, I knew. Only someone in love with her would look at her like that."

In a rush he told her, "I've got no time to waste then. Now, I have to go back in and explain to my guests that there will be no wedding today after all. Regrets and sincere apologies need to be made for any inconveniences this may have caused them. But at the same time, I don't dare reveal too much, as I don't want to start a panic. Therefore, Amy, I want you to keep away from people as much as possible. Please only tell both her father and mine. Also, that I'll explain to them later.

"Now, while I talk with the guests, I want you to take this message to Mac. He should be out in the yard by now, instructing his men for the ceremony. He's the big one with the head of shockingly red hair. Tell him to form an entourage of fifty of my best men and meet me at the stables with the horses saddled and ready to go. He'll know what to do when you tell him what's happened. But say nothing to anyone else. We must search the entire area immediately. I want this thing kept hush-hush for now," Colwyn reminded her.

With a quick nod of his head to Amy, Colwyn hurried back inside with a heavy heart.

Amy ran as fast as her fat, stumpy legs would carry her, knowing she needed to do his bidding and do it quickly. He had entrusted her to get this job done, and by golly she determined that she would and before he could say jackrabbit.

With some trepidation, Colwyn faced his guests. This was not how he had planned to face them only a short time ago. Though he was not looking forward to the announcement he had to make, he knew he had to get it over with before leaving in just a few short minutes to scour the area for Lysette.

Upon his entrance, the gathered crowd turned in their seats in expectation. "Family, friends, and honored guests," he began his explanation. "I have an announcement to make. First, I must inform you that there will be no wedding today."

The crowd was immediately in an uproar and Colwyn

had to waste precious minutes in his endeavor to settle them down.

"Folks," he continued, "please be quiet for a moment while I explain." Immediately, they stopped chattering and listened intently.

"Something has come up and I must be gone for awhile. I apologize for any inconvenience this might have caused you. You're all welcome to stay as long as you like or need to. For now, I thank you for your kindness and consideration, but I must be off."

Without waiting to answer any of the many questions the crowd individually and collectively was asking, he turned around and was gone just as fast as he had appeared.

A general mixture of feelings—concern, worry, fear and curiosity—came from the crowd as soon as he was out of sight. On the lips of most was the question, "Had the lovely young newcomer jilted the next Earl of Camden, and if so, why?" All were baffled at what could have gone wrong on this most perfect of days—that is, all except one.

Felicia Buchanan sat in her seat with a very self-satisfied evil smirk on her face. She didn't have to ask anyone or wonder, for she knew exactly what had gone wrong.

At that very moment, Colwyn was mounting his steed while all manner of horrible images filled his head. Desperately he tried to push those thoughts from his mind but in spite of his determination, they kept intruding. Since they wouldn't retreat, he asked himself the dreaded question, *Could she have met with foul play?* He prayed it wasn't so. Then, another horrible thought came to mind. One he dared not dwell on because of what it could do to his heart. *Dear God! Could she have run from me again?*

2

JEREMY KEMP HAD BEEN ASSIGNED kitchen duty earlier that day, not normally part of his duties but with the wedding and many invited guests they needed every available extra pair of hands. Usually he worked in the stables, taking care of the horses, which he preferred. For a gangly boy of eleven, he was still somewhat clumsy, but always very eager to learn.

Both of Jeremy's parents had been servants of the Campbell family, so that meant he had been born into servitude. Teresa, his mother, had died giving birth to him; so tragically, he had never gotten to love her or to even know what she looked like. According to his father, Jonathan, he had only a description of her and the assurance that she was the most beautiful and kindest woman he had ever known. That was information that Jeremy always kept close to his heart.

To make the poor lad's situation even worse, his father had been killed in a horrible accident in the stables when a horse he was tending suddenly became spooked and trampled him to death. Jeremy had been only seven at the time and had suddenly found he was an orphan.

Cook (or Cookie to those who were close to her) and her husband, George, who was the head grounds keeper at the castle, were the only ones who knew Cook's real name and had vowed to take it to their graves. For years they had tried unsuccessfully to have children and to their sorrow, had to accept that Cookie was barren.

They felt sorry for little Jeremy's plight and now, in their mid-forties, there was a child who needed them. There was some concern that at their age they might have a bit of a problem keeping up with him. But, since they already loved him so much, there really was only one thing they could do—go to the Earl and ask him if they might raise him as their own. This they did and of course the Earl granted them permission. Ever since, Jeremy had had a loving family and he in turn was a happy boy who loved his parents dearly.

On that particular, most special and very hectic day, Cook had ordered him down to the cellars to fetch a bucket of flour from the barrel as she had planned to make her mouth-watering fruit pastries for dessert. Unfortunately, he had filled the bucket a little too full for his slight build to handle. Just as he reached the last stair at the top upon his return, his foot tripped on the landing thus spilling the entire contents of the bucket all over the floor. Then to make matters worse, while he had been trying to clean up the mess, he again fell in the slippery flour. As he fell, he hit the side of the kitchen table, knocking off all the bowls sitting on top. Thus, their contents combined with the flour that was already on the floor.

"Ahhh!" Cook screeched. "Just look at this mess ye've made!" And she promptly proceeded to box his ears—not too hard though, for her heart wouldn't allow that.

"It'll take me forever and a day to clean up all this. Why ye're a walking disaster, boy! Git now from me sight a-fore I really lose me temper!" she exclaimed while she shooed him out the back door with her heavy Scottish brogue. This was no time for him to make more of a mess.

Though she worried about being too hard on him, right now she needed him out of the way.

Jeremy wasted no time after that. He ran from the kitchen holding his ringing ears not even thinking of where he was going. It was pure instinct, as he headed in the direction of the gardens, his most favorite place in the world. They always helped to soothe his troubles and put him in a tranquil mood. The flowers were so beautiful and smelled so lovely, a welcome change from the stench of the stables he usually had to smell all day. But he never dared tell anyone of his little secret, as he feared they would poke fun and accuse him of being unmanly.

It had been Mistress Elizabeth's favorite place also. When she had come there from England, one of the first things she'd asked of the Earl was that the garden be put back in order. Since she loved flowers so very much, she had balked at the sight of the neglect and the overgrown weeds. Especially right before she was to marry the Earl's son. Soon after their marriage, you could find her puttering away out there getting just as filthy as any of the help.

Many times Jeremy would help her after he had finished his work in the stables. Therefore, he had had developed a deep love for the gardens. Also, he was very glad they were positioned down wind of the stables as it helped staunch the stench. He knew he would always cherish those memories of working side-by-side with the mistress.

Still feeling miserable about his recent fiasco in the kitchen, Jeremy was sitting on one of the benches, daydreaming, when he heard a noise not too far from him. Quickly he crouched down behind a hedge of bushes, fearing discovery.

After a few moments, he decided to take a discreet peek through a small opening in the hedge in order to find out what had made the noise. Upon seeing her, he recognized her at once as Felicia Buchanan's maid. He wasn't too fond of her because she was always so mean and hateful to him. Briefly he wondered, *What pried her from Felicia's side since one is hardly seen without the other? A stranger pair I've never seen.* He didn't have long to wonder though, as he spotted her mistress arriving a short time later.

"Why have you come alone?" Felicia hissed at Elsbeth. "Could you not convince her to speak with me? Didn't you tell her I wished to apologize?" Felicia was becoming very impatient by this time and in exasperation said, "Hell's breath, Elsbeth! This would be my only opportunity and I must not fail. She *must* be standing before me."

"That's the beauty of it, I didn't have to," Elsbeth answered when she finally had her chance to speak. "The fates are smiling down upon us this day."

Devilishly pleased with their evil conspiracy, Elsbeth continued her tale. "It seems Lysette is feeling a tad nervous and has wedding day jitters. I overheard her telling her maid, while I was mingling with the servants in her dressing room, that she wanted to go out to the gardens in order to be alone for a while. That was when I slipped out to warn you. I don't think she left far behind me so should be here any moment."

"Good!" Felicia replied gleefully. "Things couldn't be working out any better. Did you bring the wine?"

"Yes!" Elsbeth answered, as she held out the glass to Felicia. "I grabbed one from the tray on the table before the servant came to pass it around to the guests."

"Quickly hand it over to me, so I can pour in the potion," Felicia commanded. "Then you go hide over there behind the bushes," she told her maid, pointing to the ones opposite to where Jeremy was hiding. “We wouldn’t want to overwhelm her and scare her off by the both of us standing here waiting, now would we?” she smirked.

Jeremy breathed a sigh of relief when he saw Felicia point in the opposite direction of where he was hiding. Initially, he had been concerned that the two women might have heard him. Then he watched as the maid handed the wineglass over to her mistress, who then took a vial that had been hidden under her cloak and poured the entire contents into the glass. However, he had trouble making out exactly what they were saying. Then the maid disappeared from his view.

It was only a few seconds later when the young master’s bride-to-be appeared in the doorway that lead out into the gardens. When Lysette spotted Felicia standing there, she turned to go another direction but Felicia reached out to detain her.

“Lysette,” Felicia urged pleadingly. “Wait a moment. Will you, please? I’d like to make amends for my rudeness at our meeting the other day.”

Personally, Lysette had doubts that this woman had ever felt sorry for anything she had done. But she thought to herself, *What would be the harm in hearing what she has to say? I’m not exactly looking forward to starting out my new life having a ready-made-enemy.* So ignoring her first instincts about Felicia, she shrugged her shoulders and continued into the garden to join her.

“I realize I wasn’t very friendly then,” she said rather contritely. “But, you see, I care for Colwyn quite deeply, as a *friend,* of course,” she stressed rather specifically. “Naturally, I am sure you can understand that I didn’t want to see him hurt in any way. When you arrived, you didn’t seem too thrilled about your coming marriage and I honestly thought you intended to back out of it, thus causing Colwyn possible pain and/or embarrassment. But I can see I was wrong. Colwyn seems very happy about this union and I only want what's best for him. Therefore, I would like to start over and welcome you. I hope we can be friends as well as neighbors."

Lysette still had her suspicions about Felicia's motives, but thought she sounded sincere right now. "You certainly were very cold and uncivil that day," Lysette emphasized.

"And again, I apologize for my unpardonable rudeness," Felicia amended.

"To be truthful, that day I was rather unapproachable myself," Lysette offered as an olive branch.

"It wasn't entirely all your fault we got off on the wrong foot," she went on to explain. "I took my bad mood out on everybody I encountered that day." She didn't want to impart anything more revealing than that.

"All right, Felicia. I am willing to accept your apology and offer you mine as well in return," Lysette graciously agreed.

"Well then, Lysette, I'd say the matter is settled and best behind us. Do you think we could try to be friends?" Felicia offered again.

"We could try, of course," Lysette agreed, and quickly offered her hand in friendship. Inside she still had grave doubts that she would ever be close to this woman. There was just something about her that came across as fake, and Lysette didn't completely trust her yet. She decided that at least on this, her wedding day, it wouldn't hurt to be friendly.

"You must be a little jittery about now, what with you about to become a new bride and all," Felicia said, continuing her friendly pose making unnecessary conversation by stating the obvious.

"Yes, I guess I am a little," Lysette confessed. "But I expect I'll get over it."

"Of course you will," Felicia assured her. "I have something here I think will help. Before coming out here I grabbed a little wine for myself and I haven't sipped from it yet. I'd like to offer it to you. I find that a little wine always steadies my nerves a bit when I'm a little too anxious. Why don't you take it? I think you probably need it a little more than I do at this moment."

"Yes, I noticed you holding the wine," Lysette stated. "But I wouldn't dream of taking yours. I can always get some later."

"Oh, that's quite all right!" Felicia urged. "I really don't mind as I find I would rather not have it now anyway."

Lysette realized she did feel a little parched at this time and figured it wouldn't hurt to take a little sip.

"Thank you, Felicia. That's very kind of you, but only a little bit. After all, I wouldn't want to get drunk before the ceremony," she joked a little.

Taking the offered glass from Felicia's hand, Lysette lifted it to her lips and began slowly to sip it. As she did so, Felicia suddenly lifted her arms in the air and began to shrilly chant in an unrecognizable language. Then she loudly shouted, "I call upon the dark one to rid me of this thorn in my side, so I can be free to be with the one I love!"

Lysette stood dumbfounded; a look of shock plastered on her face. She seemed frozen in place—unable to move even one small finger.

Jeremy saw the sky darken and some very threatening clouds rest overhead. But it was really strange, for the dark clouds were only over where the new mistress stood. From out of nowhere, a whirlwind of high velocity kicked up and threatened to blow the new mistress away. Sud-

seen. Everyone is inside waiting for the ceremony to begin."

"Perhaps you're right," Felicia capitulated. "I just thought I smelled something in the wind. Come on then, let's hurry inside before someone starts to miss us and comes looking." Then she practically hauled Elsbeth through the door because she wanted to quickly dismiss the feeling from her mind.

Jeremy had given a low, inaudible gasp of fright at what he had just witnessed. When Felicia had stopped and sniffed in his direction, he had crouched down lower and prayed he would not be discovered. His whole body was shaking from head to toe with fear. He gave a sigh of relief as his prayers were answered and they finally turned to depart.

Quietly, without moving for several minutes, Jeremy waited till the two women were out of sight before he dared come out from his hiding place behind the hedges. Then, he scooted off, like a hare being stalked by a fox, toward his little area above the stables. His scrawny little legs were going as fast as they could carry him.

3

COLWYN FELT AS IF HIS MIND WAS racing as fast as his steed while they tore across the Scottish moors, searching for any clue to Lysette's whereabouts. Having sent a scout to her home, he would know soon enough if that was where she had gone. If not, then she had to be in the immediate area and he trusted he and his men would soon find her.

His thoughts continued to race as he wondered, *If she has actually gone back on her word and run from me again, how had she accomplished it with absolutely no signs left behind? Did she have any help? She barely had enough time to know me, much less anyone else. No one else around here would take the risk of hiding her out and incurring the Earl's wrath. And if she had been abducted, why hadn't they left a ransom demand behind? It made no sense at all.*

He rehashed over in his mind the last two days they had spent together. To him, it had been two of the most glorious days he had ever experienced. It had been a time of laughter, and the discovery of each other's innermost thoughts and desires. Even now, he was amazed he had opened up to her as much as he had, but even more so, that she had responded in kind.

When they had first begun to ride over the vast expanse of his land holdings, their conversation had started out stiff and sparse. Then it had moved onto rather civilized subjects. Followed, surprisingly a discussion that had actually become quite easy and friendly. The amazing thing was that it had happened in such a short time.

He especially remembered, with satisfied warmth, when they had finally approached the pond where he had stopped her that first night as she had tried to escape him. How hotly she had blushed, when he had glanced over at her with a wickedly secret grin. Lysette's embarrassment was quite becoming and he felt his arousal begin as before. She had tried to ignore any reference to that enchanting night, but she hadn't fooled him though. He could tell she was remembering with excitement also.

That day, he had made a very significant discovery about himself. He had discovered he felt more contentment in her company, those last two days, than he had ever felt with anyone else. Naturally, he had been pleased when she finally had seemed to warm up to their marriage even though it was between two, almost virtual strangers. Actually, she was the one that had convinced him, she was beginning to like him.

Now, he had to wonder, *Had it all been a ruse to throw him off his guard, so she could plan her escape? And if this wasn't the case, then someone must have taken her. It was this possibility that worried him the most.* He shuddered at the image his mind conjured up of the mistreatment she might be receiving at the hands of his enemies.

* * *

It had been two solid days now that he had been searching for Lysette without any luck. To him it seemed they were no closer now to finding her since they had first started out to look for her. He had been in contact with his father through messengers sent back and forth, informing him of his progress, and inquiring of any word they might have received back home. Still, there was nothing and Colwyn had never felt more frustrated or useless in his entire life.

It didn't help to know that his father was more than angry with him for leaving without a first-hand explanation. But, he had tried to explain that he simply hadn't had the time if he was to make any headway at all. Only now, to find out that it hadn't made any real difference. His father informed him, that Asa Duncan, Lysette's father, had taken ill when he had been told of her disappearance. For now, he would convalesce at their castle and wait for word about his daughter.

Colwyn had not one single word yet to give and hated to return home empty handed. But he was bone-weary and tired from no rest or sleep over the past two days. He had driven his men and the horses too hard and they were all showing definite signs of fatigue, more and more with each passing moment. It was now time to return, refresh, and rethink his strategy, for his next move had to be soon.

In order to keep his mind from worrying about Lysette or if she was suffering from any kind of fear or pain, he concentrated his thoughts on the first time he set eyes upon her and all the past events that had eventually led up to this tragic situation—

Colwyn grimaced at his father's servant when he had handed him Angus Campbell's summons. He wanted to meet him in his study at once. The servant then added a personal note: "Lord Campbell said to tell you it was most urgent, sir."

Annoyed, Colwyn mumbled to himself, *That doesn't surprise me. It's never anything but.* Out loud he said, "Tell my father, that I'll be along in a moment."

The servant bowed his head in respect, turned, and retreated to carry out his latest order.

At the moment, Colwyn felt no alarm at this latest summons. After all, he'd been receiving quite a few lately. But he had to admit he was feeling more than slightly irritated at this one because it couldn't have come at a more inopportune time. He had just been about to oversee the needs of their tenants. Now his departure would have to be delayed.

As he shut the door to his room and proceeded down the stairs to his father's study, thoughts swirled through his mind: *Father probably wants to discuss the subject of my marriage again, and I'm just not in the mood to have him berate me because I'm still a bachelor. If I hear, one more time, how it is my duty to carry on the line and produce legitimate heirs, I'm going to shout the castle down. Besides, I'm only twenty-six years old, there is plenty of time to marry and settle down to one woman.*

Oh, well, I might as well get this unpleasantness over with as fast as I can so I can get on with my business at hand.

Angus Campbell, Tenth Earl of Camden, sat in his study contemplating his decision while he waited for his son's arrival. He assured himself for the hundredth time that he had done the right thing. Also, in his heart, he believed that his Lizzie would have approved, even though she had doted on their only child and given in to him most of the time. Now, the Earl consoled himself with the fact that though their marriage had been arranged, they had found idyllic happiness together.

Ah Lizzie, my Lizzie, how I miss you, he sighed as he thought of her just then. In his mind's eye, he could still see how beautiful she had looked the first time she had been presented to him. But now, she had been gone one and a half years this past winter, and to him it seemed more like an eternity. They had known she had had a weak heart and that's why her doctor advised her not to have any more children after Colwyn's birth. At that time she had almost died, but Angus personally nursed her around the clock, with very little rest for himself. Her doctor had been impressed with her quick recovery, but Angus was not willing to put her health in jeopardy again.

In retrospect, Colwyn has turned out to be a fine young man. A little bit spoiled and slightly headstrong, that's putting it mildly, Angus laughed to himself. He would always have his cherished memories.

Angus was fifty-three and was beginning to feel his age. Where once his hair had been coal black, it was now salt and pepper with more gray in evidence since she had been gone. He was glad Colwyn's looks took after his mother. She still had had a youthful appearance, even right before she had died.

While waiting for Colwyn, his thoughts continued in the same vein, *It is time I have a bushel of grandchildren always getting underfoot and filling this somber old castle with laughter. I want them and the sooner the better, before it is my turn to take my place in the afterlife. Just think of the happiness I could share with Lizzie when I join her and tell of all the exploits of our young grandchildren.*

But, first things first, he told himself as his mind shifted to the business at hand. *I'm not looking forward to informing my son of the arrangement I made. I know it is going to be our most explosive confrontation yet.*

Colwyn didn't bother to knock as he barged into his father's study. As he went through the door he said, without preamble, "All right, Father, I've come as you commanded. What is it this time?" He hadn't bothered to hide the irritation in his voice.

Angus ignored his son's rudeness and barked authoritatively as he pointed to a chair, "Sit down, Colwyn! I've something to discuss with you."

Colwyn disregarded the chair he indicated and still standing said, "I don't think I should, Father. If it is what I think it is, I won't be here that long."

"Sit down, Colwyn!" his father repeated, with distinctive anger apparent now. "This is not a request. It is an order!"

When his father used that tone on him, Colwyn knew it was useless. He would brook no argument from his son.

"I've been in contact with an old friend of mine from my days as a young man," his father continued talking while Colwyn took his seat. "He's head of the Clan Duncan from up in Dundee."

Uh oh, Colwyn thought to himself, *here comes the part I know I'm not going to like.*

"It just so happens, he has a daughter, just as willful and stubborn as you, especially when it comes to the subject of marriage."

I was right, this is it, Colwyn told himself.

"She's twenty years old, really quite lovely and she has refused every one of her suitors, stating she can find none that she is satisfied with."

Colwyn knew what was coming now and he was ready for his father. His demeanor was very determined as he began to rise from his chair. "You can forget it, Father," he stated emphatically. "I have no intention of meeting her and being your pawn in this whole farce!"

"You'll not only meet her," his father's booming voice, stopped him midway, "but you'll marry her in a week's time!"

"What!" Colwyn shouted in disbelief. "That is the most outrageous . . . you can't be serious! I *won't* do it!"

The look on the Earl's face did not change. It was the most determined look Colwyn could ever remember seeing on him, almost as if it were etched in stone. He knew then that there was no way his father would budge on this issue but he was determined to try anyway.

"You will!" his father loudly ordered. "I am still the Earl here and my word is law. I've given my *word* that you *will* go through with the marriage. Now, do you intend to disgrace me?" his father asked with accusation, using the emotion of Colwyn's guilty feelings, as his leverage tool to gain his son's compliance.

"But I don't know this girl," Colwyn pointed out. "How can you ask me to take her sight unseen?"

"She will be here in four days time," his father informed him. "That will give you three days; plenty of time to get to know her."

Colwyn just stared incredulously at his father. *This could not be happening. It makes absolutely no sense. It is as if my father has lost all his sensitivity. He is so adamant about this business and I can see there will just be no reasoning with him,* Colwyn thought.

"Unless, of course," the Earl added inquiringly, "you can tell me now that you prefer someone else."

"No!" Colwyn stated irritably. "You know very well that I prefer no one. I've made myself clear on that subject."

Angus let out a secret sigh of relief at this answer. He had been a little afraid that Colwyn might have said that he preferred Felicia Buchanan. Thank God, he didn't. If he had, he wasn't sure how he would have dealt with that. Though he had known Colwyn had shown an interest in Felicia in the past, he had hoped it was over.

A strange one, Felicia was. Whenever she was around, Angus could swear he felt a cold chill creeping in his bones. Since her father was one of his best friends, she had always been made welcome in his home even though there had been some speculation going around that she had had something to do with her own mother's death. The subject was never mentioned in her or her father's presence however; no one would have been that insensitive. As no proof had been found, the matter was dropped.

"I have no time for a wife now," Colwyn went on to explain. "I'm much too busy and wouldn't be able to give her the attention she deserves. You'll just have to get back in touch with your old friend and his daughter, what's-her-name, and inform them the marriage will have to be dismissed."

"I'm afraid I can't do that," Angus added certainly. "The banns have been posted and the invitations sent out. You have no choice in the matter. At the week's end, you *will* marry unless you intend to make me live with the disgrace of going back on my word," he ended effectively.

Colwyn knew when he was being manipulated, and quite successfully too. Also, he realized his father knew he had him this time, as he would never bring dishonor on the family name. The guilt would eat away at him.

"Very well, Father," he acquiesced for the time being, as he breathed out a sigh of defeat. "This time you have won the battle, but the war isn't over, yet. I have seven days in which to outwit you. I'll think of something to stop this entrapment."

That was to be Colwyn's last statement on the subject as he stormed out the door and slammed it hard. Angus let out a sigh of relief at his temporary reprieve. Actually, he had thought their fight would have lasted longer and been more furious. He couldn't help but be glad it was over for now. Then he chuckled deeply to himself and to his victory in round one.

Colwyn was fuming as sat upon the back of his stallion, Satan, and they raced furiously across the countryside. It felt good to be able to release the pent up tension he had been holding within himself. His thoughts went almost as fast as his horse and were a jumbled mass of chaos. He had just a few days to come up with a plot to put a halt to his father's scheme for him and he just couldn't think of anything feasible that his father would not see through or get around. *There must be a way to stop the arrival of my unwanted bride-to-be!* he thought in desperation.

4

SITTING ASTRIDE HER MARE, LYSETTE Duncan observed the formidable looking castle ahead. It definitely was not a welcome sight and to her it spelled doom and servitude. In the past, her father had always given her free reign over her own life but now, all of the sudden, he had inexplicably taken it away from her.

As she rode along she wondered, *Why? Was it simply because I had passed marriageable age and hadn't yet chosen a suitable suitor? It just doesn't make any sense. I don't see why things couldn't have continued as they were. Now I'll have to answer to a husband and all of my freedoms will be taken from me. Once a woman is married she has no rights. Her husband controls everything.*

With thoughts like these her future looked very bleak indeed. Wanting to be alone in her misery, Lysette had ridden a few hundred feet ahead of the wedding party. Suddenly she pulled back on the reigns of her horse bringing them to a stop as she now had neither the willpower nor the desire to go any further. Briefly she considered turning around and taking off at a full gallop but knew the idea was hopeless, as her father's men would shortly catch up with her.

Taking a moment, she observed the castle ahead of her. It was certainly grand enough with its matching tower houses, impressive battlements and turrets, plus a reinforced gate with a watchtower just above. Upon seeing it, she now better understood why her father had considered this an excellent alliance. But personally, she was not impressed as she resented being a prize to be pawned off to the highest bidder.

Even now, she still found it hard to believe her father had done this to her. If he'd only given her just a little more time, she would have finally picked someone she considered suitable, just to get him off her back. She could have made sure it was a long engagement—till she could've come up with a plan to call it off. But now, it was beginning to look as if the situation was desperate. He was giving her no time or choice.

When her father rode up and stopped beside her she entreated once again, "Father, how could you do this to me? How can you make me marry a man I've never seen before?"

Asa Duncan looked squarely into those pleading eyes, eyes so like her lovely mother's; he almost caved in, but not quite. He answered her question, yet again, for what seemed to him to be the hundredth time since he had first broached the subject to her of her impending nuptials.

"Because, my little rebellious one," he started off by replying bluntly, "thus far, you have rejected every suitor that has come to call upon you since you reached marriageable age. I'm not as well as I used to be, and I want to spend a little time with a few grandchildren before I leave for the great beyond. And the way you've been behaving, little lassie, it wasn't about to happen anytime soon.

"So the time has come for me to take the matter into my own hands and bridle that obstinate streak you've got flowing through your veins. Your mother told me soon after you were born, that I would be meeting my match in you, and she was right. Cause sure enough, just as soon as you were big enough to work that tongue in your head, you've been giving me a run for my money. I've never seen anyone more ornery in my life, except, of course, for me. You may have her looks about you, but you've got my temperament. And that's my comeuppance for being so bull-headed most of my life."

He paused and studied the castle, looming in front of them now, just over the horizon, before he continued. "Your mother would like this place. You know she would love to be with you now. I can feel her smiling down on us at this moment."

Lysette was not yet ready to give it up and vehemently stated, "You're wrong, Father. If mother were here now, she would never allow you to force me into a loveless marriage."

"I disagree, kitten," he stated quite calmly, considering her outburst. "Even though you were only twelve when she passed on, she knew you were already much too headstrong for your own good; much too stubborn to accept your one true love, even while he may be staring you straight in the face. As your mother and I knew right from the first moment we met."

Speaking of her mother caused Asa to reflect a little on his deceased wife, who had been gone, these past eight years. Monique De La Croix had been the loveliest woman he had ever seen after he had gone traveling abroad to France. In his mind he again saw her strolling down the Paris sidewalk with her plump chaperone. Her figure was petite and her smile had been alluring. Without thinking, he had rushed across the street to introduce himself at once, despite the objections of her oh-so-proper and protective companion. At the time she had only been sixteen, but one look into those deep amethyst eyes and he had been lost.

Instantly she had been charmed and flattered. Her manner had been most gracious and accepting, and from there they immediately began a whirlwind courtship. After knowing each other only six weeks, they married, and then he had brought her home to his native Scotland. She had named their daughter Lysette, after her best friend she had left behind in France.

Never had she regretted her decision to marry Asa. They had been extremely happy, right up until the day she had died.

Asa pulled himself away from his memories and addressed his daughter once more, using the pet name he had bestowed upon her when she was still a wee-babe in his arms. "And besides, my little Lissie, whoever said you couldn't fill this marriage with love?" he challenged.

Lysette didn't quite know how to answer that, as she suddenly found herself speechless with surprise. *For the first time in her life,* Asa surmised as he chuckled to himself.

"From what I can remember, young Colwyn is quite the good-looking fellow and extremely kind and generous," Asa informed her. "And with that little spitfire nature of yours, little Missy, you couldn't ask for much more than that."

"Lissie," he suddenly changed his tone to try and be persuasive, trying to coax her into a better mood, "don't judge me too harshly, before you meet the man. You know I would never make a decision concerning you that would bring you any harm. I find myself extremely fortunate that Angus agreed to this union. It is an excellent match and I'm asking you to give it a chance."

"But Father, what of *my* happiness?" she said as she batted those big misty eyes at him, giving it one last try.

Asa had to steel himself against that look then said,

"You might as well cut that out now, young lady, because it's not going to work this time. In this case, I know what's best for you and I'll not hear another word on the subject."

Lysette shrugged her shoulders in defeat and decided to herself, *I'll put it to rest for the time being at least. But he has not defeated me yet. I'll think of something to stop this farce of a wedding, I still have a few tricks and a few days left.*

They continued forward then, till they neared the castle gate and drew up short. They heard a shout from above, from the lookout guard. "Halt! Identify yourself before you gain entrance to the Castle Campbell."

Her father called up his answering bellow, "It is Asa Duncan, and my daughter Lysette who is the affianced bride of the Master Colwyn!"

"Welcome," the guard shouted back down, "you've been expected. Please enter," he instructed them. With a shout he ordered the men down below, "Open the gates! The wedding party has arrived!"

Slowly the massive gates opened and the party proceeded inside. Lysette was probably the only one with a great deal of reluctance.

A message was sent up to the castle announcing their arrival. As they approached the front entrance, the doors burst forth and Angus, recognizing his old friend, Asa, in the lead, rushed out to give them a proper welcome.

"Asa!" he exclaimed. "How delightful to see you again," he announced eagerly, as he reached up to shake his hand. "I'm so glad you made it in fine health. Your journey was a pleasant one, I trust?" he inquired politely.

"Thank you, Angus," Asa answered just as eagerly. "It's good to see you also. And yes," he continued, "our journey was quite pleasant, and *almost* uneventful." He cast a discreet sideways glance in his daughter's direction at that remark. She caught the look and pointedly ignored it.

Angus noticed the brief non-verbal exchange between the father and daughter however, and sensed the tension lying just below their polite facade. Shifting his position towards the lovely young woman he said, "This vision before me can only be your lovely daughter, Lysette. I welcome you to Castle Campbell," he included them all in his statement as he reached his hand up to Lysette in a formal introduction. "I am Angus Campbell and I hope your stay here is especially delightful, but more important, that it comes to feel like home."

Lysette glanced down at his hand reaching up to shake hers and knew she must respond in kind and grasp it in greeting. Her father had raised her never to be rude, especially to her elders who were to be her hosts.

"How do you do, Milord?" she responded respectfully. "It is an honor to meet you." *I just wish that it were under different circumstances is all,* she silently added to herself.

"Tch, tch," Angus clucked. "None of that 'Milord' stuff. It is Angus to you."

"Thank you, Angus," she tried to smile sincerely as she tested the use of his given name, "I'll consider it a privilege."

"And this is my son, Colwyn," Angus introduced, as he heard the familiar clop of his son's boots coming out the door behind him, "who has been anxiously awaiting your arrival."

Upon hearing this last remark, Colwyn felt desperately like giving his father a kick in the rear. But instead, he looked up and beheld what he considered to be the most exquisite creature on God's green earth. The beautiful face was framed by raven black hair that seemed to shine blue in the sunlight as it fell in billowy waves across her shoulders and down her back. Her cheeks had a natural blush and her lips were full and shapely with a cherry-red hue, just begging to be kissed. When he met her violet eyes, they were flashing fire at him, which would have put the deepest hued amethyst to shame.

Next, he noticed her riding habit matched the exact shade of her eyes and it fit her shapely form perfectly, with lace ruffles surrounding the edge of the low-cut neck and the end of her sleeves. As his eyes traveled lower, he had to wonder how such a slender figure supported such well-endowed breasts. He noticed her waistline was cinched in tight, revealing it to be small enough for a man's hands to span. Her jewelry was simple, yet elegant, as she was wearing an amethyst and diamond broach with matching dewdrop earrings and bracelet.

Having observed her for only a short moment, he quickly masked the surprised delight on his face, at the enchanting picture she presented, staring down at him with a rebellious defiance that could easily have matched his own. This one definitely was not a desperately-seeking-a-husband-simpering-little-miss type, as he had originally imagined in his thoughts. She was definitely something entirely different. The way she was looking at him now, it was as if she'd like to skin him alive and leave his carcass to rot.

Instead of feeling irritated as he should be, he was instantly amused. *This relationship should definitely prove to be an interesting one,* he surmised to himself.

Colwyn belatedly remembered his manners after studying her so intently, and stepped in closer to get an even better view of her and politely said, "How do you do, Milady? It is a pleasure to meet you." He bowed rather chivalrously and offered his hand up in greeting.

Lysette observed his hand, held in mid-air waiting for her response. Manners dictated she needed to respond so she reached her hand down, fully intending it to be as brief a contact as possible. But to her dismay, found it taken in a firm grip and drawn to his lips. She offered no words in acknowledgment, just briefly nodded her head and quickly jerked her hand back as soon as his lips left it. Anyone observing her reaction might have been excused from thinking that his touch had scalded her.

Colwyn recognized the obvious slight for what it was and couldn't disguise the annoyance he felt from clearly showing on his face. Noticing his anger, Lysette was pleased. That way, he couldn't guess at the turbulent emotions racing through her veins at her first sight of him and reaction from his touch.

Actually, she had drawn a sharp breath after he had first stepped out from behind his father and had prayed no one had heard or noticed. But unbeknownst to her, that wasn't the case as someone hidden in the shadows had observed every move she had made.

Never in her entire life had Lysette seen a more handsome man than Colwyn. He stood well over six feet and had strong, sinewy muscles over his arms and chest that could be seen rippling under his shirt. From the looks of him he obviously was no glorified dandy who let others do all the work. His hair was a dark auburn and a little overlong as it fell in waves to the tops of his shoulders and she decided it gave him a decidedly virile look. Next, she noticed that his eyes were an emerald green, and the thought occurred to her that if they were pools of liquid fire, she would definitely fall in and drown there. A small cleft in his chin gave him a roguish appearance. And his profile seemed to be chiseled from a master sculptor—all perfect lines and angles. Since he was dressed for riding, he wore a white silk shirt that was unbuttoned enough for her to see an expanse of chest hair poking through, form-fitting tan riding britches and highly polished riding boots.

In order to rid herself of his image, she turned her head away to concentrate on what the Earl was now saying to her. He started to introduce her to someone else now, a woman, he was guiding out of the shadows of the entrance. She was fair, petite, and blonde, with ringlets hanging down her back. Her eyes were small and brown and they would have appeared to be quite bland actually, if it hadn't been for the hatefulness clearly shining out from them. And they were pointed directly at Lysette. What surprised Lysette the most, though, was the disgust written all over the girl's face! She didn't even try to hide it as she looked directly into Lysette's returning gaze.

Unaware of the unspoken challenge, Angus explained that Felicia was a close friend and neighbor as well as one of the wedding guests.

Immediately, Lysette realized she had acquired an enemy without even trying. Briefly, she wondered what she could possibly have done to bring out this woman's antagonism, but decided not to be overly concerned, as she didn't plan on being there long enough to give a fig one way or the other.

The insipid-looking creature barely even acknowledged their introduction with a stiff nod of her head and an up-tilted corner of her mouth that could only pass as a smirk.

What had the Earl said her name was? Lysette asked herself. *Felicia Buchanan! That was it,* she thought, as she made a mental note to remember it the next time they met. She had an eerie feeling they would, even though she was already planning her own escape.

The Earl was speaking again, as he beckoned them to alight from their mounts. "Please, come inside, now," he urged. "I'm sure you'd like to rest and refresh yourselves after your long journey. Don't worry about a thing, as everything will be taken care of, for tonight we feast in honor of your arrival!"

Lysette felt relief at his words, for she was weary from time spent in the saddle and longed for a hot bath. In fact, she was so tired she even allowed Colwyn to help her dismount and lead her inside.

5

FELICIA BUCHANAN WAS NOW PAST her boiling point as she barged through the entrance of her secret room down in the dungeons. The ever-dutiful Elsbeth McGregor followed close behind.

"Elsbeth, bring me my book of spells, and be quick about it!" Felicia snarled to her servant.

She hadn't liked Colwyn's first reaction to his new fiancée the least little bit even though she had been forced upon him. Though she knew he thought he'd masked it quick enough, Felicia had observed every emotion that had passed across his face. "This little nobody cannot show up now and ruin all my well thought-out plans! They have been too long in the making. I'm going to have to do something very fast and powerful to get rid of this problem," Felicia surmised as she scurried about the dungeon.

Wasting no time in doing as her mistress bid, Elsbeth pulled the book from the shelf and placed it in Felicia's out-stretched hand.

After all, thought Felicia, with a self-satisfied grin, curving up the corner of her mouth, *wasn't I faced with a similar problem when I had to get rid of that busybody mother of mine? That witch had always interfered in my business.*

It had all been too easy really. When her mother had come down with a mysterious illness, she had played the ever-caring daughter, almost constantly by her side. All the while, she had been slowly poisoning her to death, even as she was pretending to nurse her back to health.

Now, she had been constantly in a bad mood ever since the moment she and her father had received the invitation to Colwyn's wedding. *The audacity of him to marry the first slut to come along, after all the time and effort I have invested in him!* she thought to herself.

She had been in love with Colwyn since she had been twelve years old, and he seventeen. At that time her mother had told her to give herself some time, as he would undoubtedly notice her when she was older. *A fat lot of good that had done me,* she had thought irritably. *I got older and he still acted as if I didn't exist.*

That was when Elsbeth had told her there were other ways, besides the usual ones, to go about making a man notice you and achieving your deepest desires. She had then introduced Felicia to the art of black magic. Felicia had picked it up rather quickly and Elsbeth had been very proud of her avid student. Many afternoons they would disappear down into the dungeon where they practiced their craft.

Her mother had become very concerned about Felicia's strange behavior, especially when she couldn't get a straight answer to her questions as to what the two of them were doing down there. One day her mother decided to follow them in order to find out what they were about and stumbled onto their little secret. She had been horrified and outraged at their deceptive, evil practices and quickly ordered Felicia to put a stop to it and have the room emptied and barred. Then she threatened to tell Felicia's father and have Elsbeth banished from their employ.

Felicia promptly began to cry and wail pitifully,

promising never again to practice the black arts if her mother would agree not to tell her father and allow Elsbeth to stay. Against her better judgment, her mother relented and let the matter drop.

Not long after that confrontation, Felicia's mother became ill with a mysterious malady.

Love potions were one of the first things Felicia had learned how to mix. They always managed to put Colwyn in a more amorous mood—whenever she was able to slip them into his drink, that is. The trouble was though the potions never lasted long enough for her to get a proposal of marriage from him. She was determined to find a way to make them stronger and maybe she could become pregnant the next time, as she had planned. Every other attempt had been met without any success.

Felicia came out of her reverie quickly as she turned to the page she had never had the courage to try before. She had briefly considered murdering this unwanted newcomer, as she had with her mother, but it was too time-consuming and Colwyn might mourn and feel a responsibility to investigate the cause of her death. *This way,* she decided, *was much better, as Colwyn would think that his fiancée would rather run away than marry him.* Her reasoning was that if he believed that, he would put her disappearance behind him.

"Elsbeth!" Felicia continued her curt orders. "Bring me that big cooking pot over there on the other side of the table. Then I want you to gather up all the ingredients from the shelves that I tell you and put them within my reach, and be quick about it."

Elsbeth accomplished her task in a short time, as she knew what Felicia was like whenever she got like this.

Her cruelty could be unmerciful if one didn't act quickly enough.

"There's one last ingredient I need," Felicia then told Elsbeth. "You'll have to go outside for this. Take that bucket over there by the door and fill it with the vilest mud you can find. It is to represent the blood of the damned."

Elsbeth escaped through the secret tunnel leading to the outside. Once, this room had been used as a secret hide-a-way for the inhabitants of the castle in case any marauding clans or enemies managed to get inside. On the other side was the torture chamber where many an unfortunate prisoner had met their death.

How ironic, Felicia thought as she waited for Elsbeth's return, *that I practice my black magic so close to where many others have suffered in the dungeons.*

She heard the rear door open and witnessed Elsbeth's return. Elsbeth then proceeded to hand the bucket of mud to Felicia. Grabbing a handful of the mud, Felicia dropped it into the pot, mixing it with the other ingredients. Then she directed Elsbeth to the far corner of the room, telling her it would be safer for her to crouch down there.

The room was dark, except where there were small, lit candles, placed strategically in a pentagram where Felicia was standing. She then started to chant in a strange dialect that was an ancient incantation. When she stirred the mixture, a cloud of black dust formed over the cooking pot. Felicia threw up her arms and a strong wind started blowing from out of nowhere. It hovered there filling the room with a strong pungent odor that became almost stifling. Elsbeth breathed it in and choked. Felicia ignored her servant as she concentrated on what she was doing.

"I call upon the powers of my master to appear in my presence!" Felicia commanded beseechingly. "I seek a favor and am willing to bargain," she told the dust above her.

The dust formed a small whirlwind becoming stronger as she spoke to it. A deep, ominous voice sounded forth that sent a chill down Elsbeth's spine. She crouched lower in her corner. Then the cloud of dust seemed to take on the shape of a face, a dark and horrifying one that could instill terror in the bravest of beings.

"Who calls upon my presence for a favor?" it asked specifically of Felicia.

"It is I, Felicia Buchanan, your loyal and faithful servant." She directed her words at the shape.

"You are aware of the conditions of a favor granted?" it stated warningly, as the mouth contorted gruesomely.

"I know of the conditions and am willing to pay the price if it comes to that," Felicia told the entity.

Since she had no intention of failing, this obstacle was just minor in her estimation. There was no way she would allow herself to be in the position to have to make that ultimate sacrifice.

"Then, state your wish of me!" the voice commanded harshly.

"I wish you to rid me of a nuisance who has suddenly intervened into my life," Felicia stated. "A woman with dark hair and violet eyes." She continued, "I want her far away from here. Somewhere she can never get back from, or better yet, into another era of time altogether. Three hundred years into the future would be nice. This I ask of you. She stands in the way of the man I want for myself. She must be gone before the marriage takes place."

"And if I grant you this desire?" the voice asked. "What are you willing to bargain with?"

"My soul, oh evil one," she informed emphatically. "I'll give my soul free and willingly."

"You have seventy-two hours to make him yours," he granted. "If you fail, your soul is mine!" The dust then seemed to form a hand that reached out and caressed, then cradled Felicia's cheek.

"I understand," she bowed her head in reverence.

"Just call on my name again," the voice continued, "when you want this favor granted and it will be done. But be warned," the voice raised an octave, "only do so once, for after that the power will never again be granted."

After the whirlwind dissipated into thin air and the presence was gone, Felicia beckoned Elsbeth from the corner to join her. "Elsbeth, we must hurry. I want to make a potion that will erase her memory. I don't want her to remember anything about Colwyn so that she won't even have any precious memories to comfort her in the long lonely nights ahead."

She laughed so evilly, it distorted her face into something hideous to look at, as she set about her task.

* * *

Lysette was preparing for the evening's festivities with about as much enthusiasm as a snail entering a horse race. "I don't care what you lay out for me, Amy," Lysette said listlessly. "It could be a sack cloth for all I care."

"You shouldn't speak that way, miss," Amy admonished. "We need to get ya all gussied up in your best gown so you can bedazzle the breath right out of that handsome young lord."

As she spoke, Amy got out Lysette's most impressive

dress. It was a deep blue-violet silk, with a low-cut neckline and a hint of delicate lace-ruffles that would tease the viewer's eyes for a closer look. The sleeves were puffed and they also had the lace ruffles adorning the edges. The waist cinched in tight then billowed out into waves that ended at the ankles. It made her look absolutely stunning when she wore it as it emphasized her slim figure.

"I don't want to bedazzle the breath out of him," Lysette proclaimed adamantly. "This disastrous predicament is not of my doing and I just want to go home."

"I'm afraid your father would never allow that, miss," Amy answered in her no-nonsense way. "You wouldn't want to ruin his good name and bring embarrassment down on the family's honor now, would you?"

"No, I could never hurt him in such a way," Lysette answered sounding defeated for the moment.

"But Amy," she continued to make her point, "how long have you been with me?" She asked her rhetorical question knowing full well how Amy would answer.

"Why, I've been with you ever since you were a wee-little baby, miss. You know that." Amy looked at her charge as if she had taken leave of her senses.

"And in all that time," Lysette pointed out, "have you ever known me to sit back and let other people make my decisions for me?"

"Oh, no," Amy answered. "I can't rightly say that I have. You've always been a rather independent sort. I've always been so proud of you," she said, beaming her approval.

"But you can't fool these old eyes," she said, surprising Lysette. "I saw that look of interest flash in those purple peepers the minute you laid eyes on him, before you tried to mask it, that is." Amy shook her finger at Lysette as she said this, just like when she was a little girl and she had caught her in an act of mischief.

"You must admit, he is a rather handsome devil, isn't he?" Amy continued to tease her in a good-hearted manner.

"Handsome or not," Lysette used her most obstinate tone, "I didn't choose him and that's the whole point."

Granted, she thought secretively, *if we had met under different circumstances, he more than likely would have been the exact type I would have chosen for myself. But the point is moot, as that is not the case.*

Amy finished helping Lysette dress and thought she looked like utter perfection. But Lysette felt no joy in her looks. She was dreading the upcoming evening's events.

"Well, I guess I'd better go down now," Lysette uttered with a touch of melancholy. "The sooner I'm there, the sooner I can get it over with."

By the time she arrived, the banquet hall was filled to capacity. Standing there at the entrance, not knowing quite what to do next, she groaned to herself, *Plunge in headlong, or turn and flee? How am I going to make it through this night?*

Angus was the first to spot her. Quickly getting up from his chair, he hurried to her side when he had noted her hesitation. "Lysette!" he beamed as he reached for her hand. "I'm so glad you've finally arrived. Your presence just brightens up this dull old room."

Lysette thought the room was far from dull with all the colorfully dressed occupants, but refrained from saying so. She thanked him politely for his compliment, but couldn't say anything else, as she found to her dismay, her throat was suddenly dry.

Leading her to the head table, Angus seated her to his left, right next to Colwyn who was already seated.

Lysette's stomach did a flip-flop as she felt his eyes studying her. He acknowledged her presence with a slight nod of his head but refrained from speaking. Her mouth spread in a semblance of a smile before she turned away from him. Noticing the slight, Colwyn decided to ignore her for the time being. Then Angus gave the signal to the waiters standing by to begin serving the courses. There was music, entertainment, and dancing planned for a little later in the evening after they had dined to the fullest.

Lysette couldn't work up much of an appetite so she toyed with her food through every course. She felt Colwyn's eyes shift in her direction from time to time and was beginning to feel a little uneasy. Nobody seemed to be talking much, so there were long, uncomfortable silences between her and Colwyn.

When the feasting finally came to an end, Lysette desperately began looking for a legitimate excuse to cut the evening short and escape back up to her room. But luck didn't smile upon her. Angus called for the dancing to begin and asked the affianced couple to start it off. There was no way she could get out of this and allowed Colwyn to lead her out on the dance floor.

"I noticed, Milady," Colwyn broke the silence that had settled over them at the banquet table, "that you didn't seem to have much of an appetite. Not feeling well?" he inquired in a taunting way.

"Not so much a small appetite, but more a matter of the present company, Milord," she quickly retaliated.

"Ouch! That stung," he replied good-naturedly, hoping to coax her into a better mood. "Do you usually make a habit of insulting your host and shooting daggers at him through your eyes, as you are doing right now?" he teased.

"Only when I'm being forced to marry that same said host," she answered curtly.

“Touché,” he bowed to her one up-man-ship. “I guess I had that one coming, didn’t I?”

He didn’t even try to disguise the amusement creeping through his voice and dancing from his eyes.

When she continued to scowl at him with contempt, his demeanor suddenly changed and he said, “I suppose you think I am a willing participant and co-conspirator in this arranged betrothal and guess that is why you are so rude. Am I so horrible to look upon that you think I have to bargain for a wife?” he asked her with disdain. “I’ll have you know,” he continued, without giving her a chance to respond, “that I have just as many objections as to you becoming my *beloved* wife, as you have to me becoming your *beloved* husband.”

She stopped in the middle of their dance and looked stupefied as his voice increased in tempo and the crowd around them began to take an avid interest in what appeared to be the couple’s first fight.

“I want no more to do with this than you do,” Colwyn almost shouted “But you seem to hold me to blame. Unlike you, though, I can conduct myself with some manners in your presence until I can think of a way out of this mess.”

She never expected this type of reaction from him and was at a loss for words—and she was never at a loss for words! *What was happening?* she asked herself. And what made the situation worse, the music had stopped and the entire crowd on the dance floor stood there gawking at them. Since she was unprepared at how to handle this situation, she just wanted to get away and think.

When she pulled away from his loose embrace and stood staring up into his glaring eyes, she said, “I seem to have developed an excruciating headache.” This was the first excuse that had come to mind. "I beg your leave, Milord, as I would like to go up and rest now. Good night."

She made her farewell and stormed like a hurricane out of the room, leaving Colwyn standing on the dance floor alone, feeling a little foolish.

6

A LITTLE LATER, BACK IN HER room, Lysette replied with utmost assurance to her maid's remark, "No, Amy, I most definitely have *not* taken leave of my senses. This can work. I know it. I only need your cooperation."

"I don't know about this, milady," Amy responded with absolutely no confidence. "Changing clothes and all, it just doesn't seem right and you know it!" she continued with a final reprimand.

"It will be all right, Amy," Lysette assured her. "I have to wear your clothes as I could never get out of here if I wore mine. You just have to have faith in me, that's all. I'm only going home."

Home was such a safe word to her, now. She hoped when she arrived there that these strange new sensations would disappear from her mind.

When Colwyn had first taken her into his arms for the dance, she had felt a strange fluttering in the pit of her belly, like butterflies trying to escape capture. Her heart rate seemed to have tripled, and my lord, she had even begun to feel a trickle of perspiration down between her breasts. Quickly, she had to get home.

Lysette chastised herself: *I can't believe I actually stormed off and left him standing alone like that. Never before have I behaved so rudely to anyone in my life. How could he have even asked me if I thought he was horrible to look upon? He knew damn well he wasn't horrible to look upon! He is the most handsome man I have ever seen and the only one to cause me to react this way. Never before have I been stupefied into speechlessness and I didn't like the way it made me feel . . . almost as if he were inside me and could read my mind.*

Uncertainty must have gotten such a grip on me that his attitude got right to the point where I couldn't take it anymore. That must be why I ran away like a frightened little child. Now he probably hates me more than his worst enemy. What is worse, I find I actually don't like myself much at this point either.

"But how do you plan to get out of the gate?" Amy asked, intruding into Lysette's thoughts with this valid question.

"Don't worry. I've got an idea I think might work," answered Lysette. "At least I'm praying it will."

"I still don't know about this, young miss," Amy repeated with some concern. "When the morning arrives, there will be such a stink. Your father will murder me right where I stand when he discovers you're missing and the part I played in it!" she predicted frantically. "And you know how ailing he's been feeling lately. If this don't kill him, he'll kill me. I just know it. He will, I say."

"No, he won't," Lysette assured. "Yes, he'll be angry, but he'll realize I gave you no choice in the matter. He knows how headstrong and willful I can be when I feel that I'm right and he's wrong. And don't you ever tell him I admitted that," Lysette warned teasingly. "Besides, he's awfully fond of you and wouldn't want to ever lose you," she pointed out.

Amy still looked doubtful and Lysette assured her, "You really don't have anything to worry about because I'll handle Father," Lysette stated with much more confidence than she felt.

"It's just so dangerous for a beautiful young woman to travel alone on the road, especially for that far of a distance. All kinds of evil and harm could befall you. How in all good conscience can you expect me to let you go and not tell anyone? I'll be one big ball of worry. I don't see how you cannot expect me to explode!" Amy blurted so loud she spit as she spoke.

"You know as well as I do, Amy, I am perfectly capable of taking care of myself. I will be extra careful to keep hidden in the woods if I spot any trouble. I am very self-sufficient and I'll be fine. Now, I don't want to hear anymore about worrying or trying to change my mind. Do you understand?" She finished with authority.

Amy just sighed. She knew she was fighting a losing battle, and she still wasn't convinced her mistress would be fine.

* * *

Much later that night, Colwyn tossed and turned restlessly in his bed. Every time he closed his eyes, he saw a pair of hauntingly disturbing amethyst eyes staring at him in disbelief. He imagined them smoldering with desire, as she gazed upon him just like his were doing right now as he thought of her.

Just for a moment, she had left him stunned speechless when she had turned and fled, leaving him alone on the dance floor, looking like an idiot. He had considered going after her and dragging her back, demanding an apology for her inexcusable behavior. But he rejected that notion almost as soon as it entered his mind. He knew she would never humble herself to him. All over her was written her stubbornness. The words "defeat" and "I'm sorry" were not in her vocabulary. But he would give her credit though; the little minx had a lot of courage, and more spunk than any other woman he had ever known.

Tossing the suffocating covers from his restless body, Colwyn decided to go out and get a breath of fresh air in the gardens. *Might as well,* he thought, *I'm not going to get any sleep tonight.*

The rest of the castle's occupants had finally retired so he was trying to be very quiet as he made his way through the halls and down the stairs to the garden outside. He hoped the aroma from the roses might calm his nerves enough so he could become weary and stop thinking about her.

It had been only a short while that he had been sitting on the bench enjoying a cheroot, when he noticed the figure of a woman in the distance, on the path, making her way to the stables. His interest was piqued because this was a very curious and unusual event. She was dressed in servant's garb and he could tell she seemed to be rather nervous from the way she kept turning her head back and checking behind her. Also, she was carrying a bundle used for traveling. Fortunately, he couldn't be seen from where she was because of the rose bushes. He watched as she picked up her pace once realizing she hadn't been followed.

How odd, he thought to himself, because the servants were never sent out this late to do errands. Since he didn't recognize her, he thought perhaps she worked for one of the guests. He was just about to call out and ask her what business she was up to, when he saw a lock of raven black hair escaping from its confinement under the scarf she wore on her head. At once he recognized who it was. There was only one person he knew that had hair that particular shade of color.

Why that little spitfire! He had to chuckle to himself

at her bit of gumption even though at the same time he felt a heated anger rising up in him that made him long to wrap his hands around her pretty neck and ring the infuriating life from her.

What in the world is she up to now? he asked himself. As his eyes followed her every move, he stomped out his cheroot. Then, he decided he'd better follow her at a discreet distance and find out more about why she was being so mysterious.

Lysette found her mare, Sable, in the stall quickly enough, as she called out to her softly and heard her answering whinny. She had to calm her somewhat, as Sable had become a little excited upon seeing her mistress. Hoping she hadn't made too much noise, she didn't want to wake any of the help she knew were sleeping in the loft above. But, she was able to lead Sable out of the stall after she had saddled her, by gently pulling on her reins. They then walked through the stable doors.

Lysette was thankful she was able to accomplish her task without too much fuss, or anyone discovering her intentions. She hoped her escape attempt tonight would be successful. Once outside, she went to the mounting block and hoisted herself up onto Sable's back. Then situated, she steered Sable in the direction of the watchtower by the gate. *Well this is it,* she thought with a sigh of relief mixed with a queer feeling of regret that she didn't want to dwell upon. *It is now or never as my mind is made up.*

The guard called down from his watchtower post when he noticed the lone figure approach the gate on horseback. "Ho there, who are ye and what is yer business, to pass through the gates at this late hour? I've received no word of anyone departing."

"I'm the lady Lysette's maid, Amy," Lysette shouted

her lie up to him. “She has fallen desperately ill and I must seek out a healer in the village.”

“This is highly unusual, madam,” the guard responded. “Why are ye alone? Where is your escort and why not send a messenger for the doctor?” he questioned reasonably, despite his suspicions.

“There is no time to wait for an escort,” Lysette responded, managing to sound urgent and a little breathless. “She has had this illness before and we nearly lost her. I can advise the doctor of her symptoms and inform him of the treatment her doctor from home used to save her. I really must hurry.”

Using a pleading tone to give the guard an extra nudge in hurrying her along, she added to reassure him, “There will be a messenger coming up behind me to provide an escort. They shouldn’t be long in coming as they were delayed for a short time.”

She was hoping her little lie would buy her some time before he realized no one else was coming and the alarm would be sounded. “I won’t be alone for long,” she continued her persuasion. “Or would you like to be the one to explain to his lordship why you detained me while his fiancé was lying near death? If anything should happen. . . .” she drew the words out as she left that thought unfinished, hoping her craftiness was enough to incite him to go against his better judgment.

It worked. “All right,” he rasped out gravely as he gave the signal to raise the gate. He certainly didn’t want to take the chance of angering the young master as he’d never heard of anyone who could stand up to it. Besides his father, the Earl, that is.

“You may pass. But there better be someone along behind you any moment now. I can’t have a woman out alone on the roads after dark for very long. It just wouldn't do," the gatekeeper said almost to himself as he shook his head from side to side.

Lysette let out a sigh of relief that she was able to pull off her escape and dashed through the opening before he could have second thoughts and change his mind.

Colwyn sat on his stallion, Satan, back in the shadows, well hidden as he witnessed the whole exchange at a distance. *I must remember to add ingenuity to my list of Lysette's personality traits,* he told himself. *I don't ever recall meeting a woman who could continue to shock and amaze me like Lysette. She manages to run circles around me at every turn. Now that I know I'm in for the ride of my life, I must always be on my toes from now on. Funny, that pleases me more than I thought it would.*

Urging Satan out of the shadows, Colwyn slowly approached the gate. When the guard noticed him, he was more than a little surprised because he had expected one of the squires or messengers to follow behind the woman. He would have thought the young lord would be at his fiancée's bedside.

"Oh, tis you, milord," he called down to him. "I'm glad you're here. Something unusual just . . ." he began his explanation, but didn't get to finish

Cutting him off, Colwyn said, "I'm aware of the situation and it's all right, Carl." He had used the guard's name in order to reassure him and make it more personal. At first he had felt a little angry with the guard for letting Lysette leave unescorted without getting confirmation. Since he had witnessed, firsthand, her powers of persuasion, Colwyn decided to forget the guard's blunder. Besides, he knew Carl was a softie for a pretty face. "I'm the lady's escort tonight and will personally see to her safety."

"That eases me mind to hear that," Carl responded jovially. "She couldn't be safer with anyone else."

"Why thank you, Carl, for the compliment. You're performing an excellent job. Keep up the good work." Colwyn then saluted in parting as he passed through the rising gate.

"Why thank ye, young master," Carl said, now grinning from ear to ear. "Tis always a pleasure to serve you."

Colwyn picked up Lysette's trail in record time, making sure to stay far enough behind to avoid detection. From the direction she was heading, he came to the conclusion that she was on her way back to her home in Dundee.

So, she is running away to avoid this marriage, he surmised to himself, as he stopped his horse and pondered over his turbulent emotions while he watched her up ahead. *It sure would be a solution to the problem I had to face just a few days ago, if I turned around and just let her go.* But somehow, he just couldn't let her do it. His feelings had changed about the marriage and he couldn't quite pinpoint how or when that had happened. Possibly it had been the exact moment when he had first looked into those eyes and had felt lost, yet found, precisely at the same time.

In the distance he watched her near the pond and decided she had gone far enough. He had better put a stop to her hi-jinx right here and now.

Clucking to his mount, Satan picked up his pace just enough to catch up with Lysette. Obviously, she assumed her escape was free and clear by now because she no longer checked behind her for followers. Silently the horse and rider closed the distance until they came within her hearing distance. It was then that Colwyn decided to make his presence known to her.

“How far did you think you would get before someone found out and caught up to you?” he asked in a booming voice.

The sound of his voice startled her so much that Lysette practically jerked all the way around in her saddle. “Damnit!” was the expletive that left her mouth as she looked at him and discovered who owned the voice that had caught her.

For one split second though, joy had leapt into her heart, glad that it was him—the man she was unable to keep from her thoughts ever since she had first set eyes on him. Quickly, she rejected that troubling emotion and masked it with anger over her capture instead.

Frantically she was thinking, *Why didn’t I hear his approach? Did he move as silently as the clouds?* She was so intent on looking back at him, that she didn’t realize Sable had continued to move forward and was headed right for a low hanging tree branch in the pathway.

Colwyn’s warning came too late, as she was knocked off her mount and unceremoniously dumped into the murky cold pond. Trying to stifle a laugh, he just couldn’t manage it as he laughed heartily at the hysterical picture she presented sitting up to her waist in water.

“Oh! You! You!” she sputtered indignantly as she flayed her arms in the water, splashing about. “You did that on purpose, didn’t you?” she accused him loudly. “I can’t believe you’d be this mean!” He didn’t deny her accusation as he sat on his mount doing nothing.

“Well, don’t just sit there laughing your silly fool head off. Since you’re the cause of this mishap, you can come in here and help me out,” she challenged.

“Believe me, Milady,” he still couldn’t keep the laughter from his voice as he finally recovered himself enough to respond, "if I had chosen to be mean to you, it would not have been done in this manner."

He then dismounted from Satan and proceeded to walk into the pond to fetch her, paying absolutely no heed to his expensive boots and britches. Then he scooped her up into his arms as if she were light as a feather. Now, she had no choice but to wrap her arms around his neck and hold on tightly. Actually, she was a little dumb-founded and at a loss for words as she gazed into his eyes while he carried her.

When he let her down gently as they reached the bank he said, "You'll have to get out of those wet clothes immediately. With the chill of this night air, you'll catch a cold quickly," he broke the silence that brought her out of her stupor.

"I can't change here!" she expounded shrilly. "It's right out in the open!"

"This is no time to play the modest little maiden," he reasoned sensibly while he cringed at the shriek irritating his eardrums. "And besides, it isn't as if I've never seen a lady in her undergarments before."

"Oh! I can just bet you have," she replied with sarcastic anger. "But I can assure you, if she were with you, she was no lady!"

Again he just laughed heartily at her insult and pointed out in merry retaliation, "Look who's being vicious now. But, there's no need to worry. I promise I will not ravish you where you stand."

"Well, I can't undress with you standing there watching," she told him as she stomped her foot.

"Okay, if it'll make you feel better, I'll turn around and face the other way. I'll just get the saddle blanket from my horse for you to use to dry off with when you're finished. It may be a little rough but it's all I have to offer.

You'll just have to make due I'm afraid, your highness," he added with a smirk.

She chose to ignore his sarcasm for now, waiting until he had busied himself with retrieving the blanket before she proceeded to her task. She was fuming underneath her breath at the predicament he had caused. Now, she had no choice but to do as she was told.

While she was undressing, she thought to ask him, "How did you happen to find me so fast anyway? I waited until the castle had retired for the night and when I saw no one about I was very careful and slipped outside."

"Oh, I was outside in the garden when I saw you slip outside into the darkness and head toward the stables. Having found myself in a wrestling match with my covers and losing, I decided to grab some fresh air outside and smoke a relaxing cheroot. Unfortunately for you my garden has an unobstructed view of the stables. So you see, my dear, you never had a chance," he offered as an explanation.

Much to her annoyance, he sounded far too self-confident and she grimaced at her misfortune.

While she continued to undress in silence, she sulked at his untimely luck and asked herself, *Why was everything disrupting her plans?* By the time she had stripped down to her chemise, she harrumphed, deep in her throat to gain Colwyn's attention. When he turned around, he stared as if he were frozen in time. For there in the moonlight she stood, looking like an ethereal angel that had descended from the heavens. *All she was missing was her halo,* Colwyn thought.

"Well! Are you just going to stand there staring, letting me freeze to death, or are you going to toss me that blanket?" she asked irritably. She felt entirely too self-conscious with him staring at her.

Colwyn shook himself out of his trance as her words broke the spell he was under, and spurred him into action.

Lysette watched him walk towards her, and wondered why he didn't just hand her the blanket instead of walking on around her to wrap her up in the blanket himself.

The womanly scent of her went directly to his senses, faster than the most intoxicating wine. Her soft creamy shoulders were like velvet to his touch and despite his promise not to ravish her, he just couldn't help himself, and he bent to rain soft, caressing kisses on her shoulder and in the crook of her neck.

At his first light touch, Lysette's breath seemed to stop and her knees started to buckle. There was that queer feeling again, starting in the pit of her stomach and a chill went up her spine. She shivered, but not from the cold.

As Colwyn wrapped his arms about her and drew her down to the soft mossy, dew-filled ground the blanket fell from around her, forgotten in his passion. He pulled aside the strap of her chemise and started kissing lower and lower. His swift intake of breath indicated he had exposed one full soft breast at last. Then, he gently lowered the other strap until both soft, full breasts were exposed to his view.

To Colwyn, her nipples were like twin rosebud peaks, opening up to the bee for pollination and he couldn't resist a taste of her nectar. Drawing one of the buds into his mouth, he began to gently suckle. Lysette was lost in delicious languor, emotions and feelings she had never dreamed of washing over her. She found she could not utter one word of protest even as he was driving her wild.

No man had ever touched her like this. But God help her, she found herself yearning for more.

Slowly he continued to inch her chemise lower and lower as his lips followed a trail to her navel. There, he swirled his tongue around the outside and then darted it in and out. There was a sharp intake of breath as Lysette sharply reacted to the shock of what he was doing to her; but she didn't push him away. Instead, she began to squirm and found her fingers threading through his beautiful hair, drawing him closer. His hand reached down to her long leg and then began to inch higher and higher until he was inside the folds of her chemise where he found her most secret, intimate self and slipped his fingers inside the moist lips. Lost in the swirl of emotions and feelings Lysette found her legs opened to accommodate him of their own volition. All she wanted was to feel more and more of these mind-numbing sensations.

He caressed the bud of her womanhood; causing Lysette to grasp the back of his head and arched into his hand. Pulling the chemise even lower before she could think straight, he soon had it completely off, thus exposing her luscious body to his hungry gaze.

His lips followed a trail where his fingers had gone before. He began by nibbling little love bites along the inside of her thighs, driving her crazy. Soon, he had inched closer to her very private self and she could feel his hot breath tickling her skin. She bit her knuckle to keep from crying out.

Lysette was shocked to the very base of her core when in a sexual haze she realized what he was about to do next. Becoming alarmed at the intensity of her feelings she began to pull away from him saying, "No, Colwyn! Stop! We mustn't continue this. I hardly know you and despite what you must think, I am not a loose woman!"

Her reasoning seemed to bring him back to at least partial sanity and he realized that if she hadn't stopped him, he would have taken her right there on the soft ground.

"I'm so sorry, Lysette," his voice came out in a hoarse rasp. He was horrified at his unforgivable actions and what he had almost done. "Please forgive me! I lost control and overstepped my boundaries. You must think me a disreputable rake. The truth is that I've never acted that way before. I don't know what came over me, but I promise I will never treat you with such disrespect again. We'll be married in a couple of days and then I'll make it up to you. I swear by all that is holy."

Lysette was troubled at his mention of their union and said, "Colwyn, we need to talk about the marriage alliance. We cannot allow our fathers to get away with this. Since we did not agree, this farce has gone on long enough now. . . ."

Colwyn found he liked the sound of his name on her lips, but with a sense of foreboding, he knew he wouldn't like what he was sure she would say next.

"Before you say anything else, Lysette," he interrupted her, "hear me out. I've never been one to believe in love at first sight, but I felt something for you the first time I laid eyes on you that I've never felt for *anyone* else. I don't know if it's love, but it's far different from what I'm familiar with and I'd like to find out. And if you're honest with yourself you'll admit you felt something too."

Lysette didn't like him guessing her feelings so soon, so she made a sound of protest, but Colwyn stopped her again. "I'm serious, Lysette. I want to get to know you. Hell, I want to know everything about you. I want you near me. I want to see your face first thing in the morning. I want you waiting for me to come home at the day's end, but most of all, I want to make love to you till you cry out for mercy and even then I can't guarantee I'd be able to stop. If that isn't love, it's close enough to it for me. Lysette, I've never asked any woman to be my wife, or share my life. So what do you say, Lysette? Will you give us a chance? Will you marry me?"

Lysette was speechless for a few moments at his admission mainly because it was totally unexpected. She had scoffed at the idea of love at first sight herself, but had to admit, Colwyn did stir feelings in her she had never known existed. But still, she wasn't ready to identify it as love.

"I'll stay for the next couple of days," she agreed. "But only to get to know you better. If at the end of those two days I find that we're not right for each other, will you let me go without any trouble?"

"I'm afraid I'm already too far gone for that," Colwyn confessed "Make no mistake about it, I feel in my heart that you are already mine. I'll cherish you forever and do my utmost to make you happy. But if you ever leave me again, I'll come after you, *every time,* and go *any place* to find you. Remember that!"

7

LYSETTE WAS TAKEN ABACK BY his unexpected declaration, but secretly not at all displeased. She knew she could get used to seeing that handsome face in the first light of day but wasn't about to tell him that—at least not yet, anyway.

"We must get back now," Colwyn spoke clearly indicating he was giving her no other choice. "Do you happen to have a change of clothing in that bag you are carrying?" he suddenly asked.

"Of course," she scoffed at his incredibly dense question. "After all, I was on my way back to my home, as you might have guessed. It's over there still hanging on Sable," she indicated by pointing to her mare.

"I suggest you get dressed while I gather up your wet things and put them in my saddlebag."

Lysette dressed in a hurry as he busied himself with retrieving her items of clothing, being careful to keep his back to her all the time.

When dressed and ready, they rode back awhile in silence until Lysette finally broke the thick atmosphere that surrounded them saying "It'll be awfully embarrassing to go back through the gate."

"For who, you?" Colwyn chuckled as he teased her. "Certainly not for me," he ascertained needlessly then turned in his saddle to look back at her and studied her red-faced countenance. He then took pity and decided to put an end to her discomfort.

"We'll go through a secret underground passage. Later, I'll give an explanation to my guard. He is a good man and knows how to be very discreet."

Lysette was puzzled at this declaration but vastly relieved and grateful for his consideration.

Colwyn led her to the entrance of the tunnel that was hidden by an abundance of tall trees and overgrown bushes. If one did not know of its existence, it would be extremely difficult to spot. It had been built as an escape route for any family members, or servants, to flee from any enemies who might have gained access to the castle.

He tied up the horses on a big tree nearby, reminding himself to remember and ask the guard to come back here and retrieve them after he had deposited Lysette back where she belonged. Carefully, he parted the prickly bushes to make a way for them, but still the getting through was rough. Lysette felt the scratches from several bushes brushing against her skin.

Colwyn chose then to speak again as he led the way. "Don't go thinking that since I've shown you this, you can use it to escape again undetected. I'll have it guarded from now on," he warned her.

Lysette just made a face at his comment.

It was hard for Lysette to make out anything in the darkness, but Colwyn seemed to know where he was going. Soon, he found a torch that had been placed in the wall sconce and lit it.

"Follow me and watch your step," he barked out the order, then softened his tone, as he really hadn't meant to come across so harsh. "I wouldn't want you to trip and harm yourself."

Lysette followed him slowly and carefully as he

ripped through cobwebs covering the way. Obviously, the passageway had not been used in quite some time. Lysette found herself praying they would not come across any furry little creatures running around her feet.

At that moment, to her surprise, he scooped her up into his arms and carried her up the back stairs that led to the third floor hallway.

She began to protest the second she was lifted saying, "Colwyn, put me down. I mean it now. I am not an invalid. I am perfectly capable of walking the rest of the way."

"Not on your life, you prickly rose," he told her with an impish grin. "I'm beginning to like the feel of you in my arms."

And to prove it, he held her all the more tightly. She decided to give up fighting, as it was quickly apparent this man was used to having his way in most things.

As it so happened, the secret passageway was not far from her room and she laughed at the irony of the situation. If she had only known, she might have made good her escape, and would not be in this man's arms right now.

Colwyn seemed to guess at her train of thought and laughed along with her. He had taken a risk showing her the location of the secret passageway because he had a sneaking suspicion she had already guessed he would not keep it guarded. Smiling seductively, he showed he trusted her word not to run again. Lysette interpreted his smile correctly and was moved by his faith in her. Then he set her down gently in front of the door to her room.

"Will you go riding with me tomorrow . . . early?" he asked her spontaneously as he discovered he was anxious to spend the next few days alone in her company. Especially, since she had agreed to give them a chance.

"I can have Cookie fix us a picnic lunch and we can share it by the pond."

To his delight he witnessed a becoming blush spread across her cheeks.

"Yes, I think I might enjoy that very much," she teased playfully, trying not to let him guess her embarrassment.

"I'll see that you do," he teased back.

She turned to go inside, but before she could make it, he grasped her chin with his fingers and his eyes held her hypnotized as he leaned in closer. The clean, masculine scent of him wafted over her senses as she fell willingly into his embrace.

The kiss started softly at first, and then grew in its intensity to an urgent demand. His tongue slipped inside and began to play with hers. At first, she was momentarily startled and tried to pull away. But he held her more firmly and she soon found herself responding in kind. Initially, the sensations caused by tongue-to-tongue action, was a little weird and more than a little unexpected, but soon it turned into something quite exhilarating. So instead of pulling away, she tried to get closer to him. Just when she decided she liked it, he let her go so quickly she almost fell onto the floor.

"Until tomorrow then," he whispered a husky caress.

While she stood there in a speechless state, he pushed something into her hand. Then he was gone. Looking down, she noticed they were the wet clothes she had worn as a disguise. She had forgotten all about them. Puzzled, she thought, *When had he retrieved them from the saddlebags? I never even noticed. That man definitely can mess with my common sense.*

Upon walking into her room, she found Amy anxiously in there waiting. When she saw it was Lysette, she was so relieved that her mistress was back safe and unharmed, that she rushed to her joyously. Lysette stopped the massive motherly arms from engulfing her in a bear hug by handing her the wet clothes. Amy stood there with her mouth wide open, not knowing what to make of Lysette's strange behavior.

"I'll explain it all in the morning," Lysette offered to clear up her maid's confused mind.

Amy just shook her head, staring stupefied at the mess in her hands, giving up any attempt to try and understand. She had never before been so glad to see anyone in her entire life.

Colwyn couldn't wait to get a fresh start with Lysette early the next morning. When he woke up, he was wearing a big grin on his face. He thought to himself, *If I had been born a female, the only way to describe my feelings right now would be 'giddy as a little girl' and that is preposterous. I have never been giddy a day of my life.*

He attended quickly to his toilette and dressed in a hurry. His intention was to get down to the kitchen early and ask cook to prepare a very special picnic basket for today. It had to be perfect even if it took most of the morning to prepare.

Willing to do anything for the handsome young man, cook prepared a baked chicken and fresh bread, while Colwyn himself picked out the cheese, wine and fruit. Then, he went out to accomplish his usual duties and inspections. He wanted to get everything done so he could spend most of the afternoon with Lysette.

When the noon hour finally arrived, Colwyn led Lysette's mare to the front gate where they were to meet. They had decided to take their horses instead of driving the wagon because they both loved to ride horseback.

Colwyn had already anchored the picnic basket on Satan. No problem, he carried it with ease.

Lysette walked out to meet him and she was dressed in a comely, violet day dress and Colwyn drew in his breath at the picture she presented. She reminded him of a gorgeous spring day. God! He loved her in that color.

He got down to help her mount up and she flashed him her most brilliant, yet slightly shy, smile. It made him tingle from head to toe. If he had doubted it before, he now knew he was a goner as his heart was absolutely tied with her golden lasso. Surprised to find it hard to confess in words how she made him feel, he greeted her cheerfully and told her how lovely she looked.

When she greeted him back, she returned his compliment and this caused him to laugh heartily at that.

After they had both mounted, he gazed at her with those emerald eyes and asked, “Are you ready?”

She smiled at him coquettishly and answered, “Just as ready as you are!”

He cocked his head at her answer and signaled the horses to start out.

On the trip to the pond, they both were noticeably silent, yet it was not an uncomfortable one. Both were reliving in their minds what had transpired between them just the night before. Every time Lysette caught Colwyn glancing her way, a very becoming, embarrassed blush stained her cheeks. He just enjoyed watching the emotions as they played across her beautiful face.

Once they arrived at the pond, Lysette tried to help set things up, but Colwyn would have none of that. He picked a spot where the grass was the softest under a big shady oak tree. Then he pulled from the picnic basket the blanket his mother had knitted and spread it out carefully on the ground. Not wanting her to do anything, he had Lysette watch and wait while sitting under the shade of the tree. Though she felt useless, it was quite flattering that Colwyn was going through so much trouble just to impress her. Sitting there, she smiled and clasped her fingers together in order to keep from jumping up and helping him. Finally, when he had everything set up to his liking, he brought her over to sit on the blanket and served Lysette her plate. Next, he opened the wine and poured each of them a glass. The whole time she watched him in stunned silence at the polite way he was behaving towards her today—a far cry from their other encounters.

After he placed the wine glass in her delicate hand, he raised his in the air and said, "I would like to propose a toast."

"Alright," Lysette agreed as she raised her glass to meet his. "What would you like to toast?"

"I would like to toast to our fathers and the day they decided to arrange our marriage."

Lysette was sipping from her wine glass just as he declared this, causing her to involuntarily spit it out and then almost choke at the shock of his unexpected statement.

Colwyn immediately bent to help her regain her breath.

"I thought that might surprise you," he confessed.

She peered at him from her watery eyes, caused by her coughing bout and dabbed her fingers at them in order to try and wipe them up so she could see more clearly. At this point, she really didn't know what to say to him, but it didn't really matter because he didn't give her a chance as he continued, "Tell me, Lysette, with your looks, how have you managed to keep all the marriageable young suitors vying for your hand at bay and remain single all this time? I'm amazed someone hasn't snatched you up and locked away so no one else could gaze upon your beauty."

Lysette was taken aback by his question but decided to answer him anyway. "It hasn't happened because I choose my destiny and I run my own life, and always have! That is to say, I always *did* until my father dragged me here and informed me otherwise. Besides, I could ask you the same question," she threw back at him.

"Are you saying that you find my looks so exceptional, that I would have had to fight off the young ladies that wanted to drag me to the altar?" he slyly asked.

Lysette's eyes rounded at her slip. She didn't want Colwyn guessing, yet, that she found him very attractive. "That is not what I said," she burst out. "*You* said that! Besides, I'm willing to concede that your looks are reasonable enough that the young ladies wouldn't necessarily run the other way."

Colwyn laughed heartily at her admission. "How is it that you have managed to slip the bonds of matrimony from your feisty little neighbor, Felicia Buchanan?" Lysette asked him suddenly as he finished his laughter. "I've seen the way she looks at you. A long time ago she set her sights on you and she views me as an unwelcome interloper."

"Felicia!" Colwyn responded in surprise.

"You must be misinterpreting her actions. I've known Felicia since she was a baby. She is like a sister to me and knows there can never be anything romantic between us. Once more, she doesn't expect it. Felicia won't be a problem for us, as I don't intend to see her as often. In fact, recently it seems as if every time I see her, I develop an excruciating headache and can't remember much of what happened. But for now, I don't want to speak of Felicia and more, let's forget all about her."

Lysette shrugged her shoulders. "If you say so," she agreed outwardly, but on the inside she felt differently. Felicia was not one to be forgotten. A queer feeling came over her and she felt sure the subject of Felicia was not one that was over. As a matter of fact, just thinking about her gave her the shivers.

"Let's talk about us," Colwyn suggested with another sly smile. "Why are you sitting so far away from me on the edge of the blanket? The air is getting a little chilly this afternoon so why don't you scoot a little closer and I'll share some of my warmth with you. I don't bite, you know. Well . . . at least not very hard," he added wolfishly.

Colwyn was beginning to feel amorous after consuming several glasses of wine during the afternoon and Lysette had observed the twinkle in his eyes. Right now, she would be willing to bet she could read his mind.

"Thank you for your offer, but I feel rather comfortable over here. I don't find the air too chilly at all."

She tried to sound distant and polite, but the sound of her teeth chattering belied her statement. "Come now," Colwyn coyly responded. "You don't have to try and be brave with me. I can see the goose bumps forming on you arms."

Lysette immediately began to rub her hands briskly across her arms to warm them up. "Here, let me do that," Colwyn offered and before she could refuse, he was there looking directly into her eyes, rubbing her arms sensuously and drawing her nearer. She felt hypnotized and her lips were moving closer to his of their own free will.

The first touch was soft and light, almost as if they were experimenting. Then the kiss deepened in intensity so deep in fact, that Lysette felt as if her head was spiraling and her soul was beginning to lose its individuality and merge with his as one whole person. She felt as if she was sinking and she wasn't quite sure why she wasn't fighting to escape.

Not breaking contact, Colwyn lay her down gently on the soft blanket, his mouth never leaving hers. As she felt his weight pressing down on her, his lips inched down her chin and neck till they came to rest at the V-point of her cleavage. There he nipped and licked teasingly and she arched her back while her arms reached up and grabbed his head.

Her hands grabbed his hair and her amethyst bracelet tangled in a few strands. The clasp broke when she tried to free it, and it fell with a thud right beside her head. Immediately, it broke the spell she was under.

"Colwyn, please," she muttered. "We must slow down. I don't think I can handle a repeat of last night."

Though in a daze, Colwyn heard her and even though his mind recognized the urgency of her plea, his body still protested. He rolled away and tried to catch his breath.

Lysette busied herself in trying to repair some order to her appearance.

Colwyn finally pulled himself together and said, "You must forgive me again, Lysette. I've discovered recently that I don't have to spend time with you for very long before I almost lose control."

Lysette didn't know how to react or respond to that, so she looked down at her side. "Oh no!" she exclaimed. "My favorite bracelet is broken."

Colwyn was immediately both relieved and grateful for this distraction. "Here, let me have a look at it," he told her while reaching down and picking it up gently off the blanket.

Within seconds, he saw the problem. "You need not be distressed, Lysette. This will be no problem at all. The clasp is merely broken and I can fix it. I will get to it as soon as I can, but I have to get it back to my room where I have a few tools. In the meantime, I have a small pouch that I keep in the inside pocket of my vest. I will just store it in there for now. That way, I will not forget it. You should have it back before our wedding day."

Lysette smiled gratefully and uttered a simple, "Thank you."

8

COLWYN DRAGGED HIS THOUGHTS FROM the memories of the past few days, back to the present as he guided Satan towards his home. He was not giving up the search for Lysette by any means, but the trail had run cold at every turn. The reason he wanted to return to the castle was he hoped he could find some answers to what had happened to her. There had to be something he had missed in his rush to find her. Over and over he told himself that he should have taken the time to investigate before he had stormed out in an all-fired hurry. If he had done so, maybe she would be back in his arms right at this very moment.

All the men, as well as Colwyn, were travel weary and dead tired by the time they arrived back at the castle late that evening. It was so discouraging that so far the search for Lysette had turned up nothing. Almost constantly he had been in the saddle, searching for clues or some kind of sign as to her whereabouts, for the past two days. Now his only hope was to find something out about her activities before she had last been seen.

Earlier that day, a messenger had been sent to her home in Dundee, in order to see if she had returned there. Colwyn had concentrated his searching in the surrounding area in case it was a kidnapping by one of his enemies. Now all he could do was to wait for the messenger to return from Dundee to find out if they had had any news.

He gave curt orders for the horses to be taken care of as soon as they approached the stables. The poor animals were feeling the brunt of the chase quite heavily by now.

As soon as Colwyn entered the stables, Jeremy Kemp was there. He had never before seen his young master look like this. Always, he had had a friendly smile and a cheerful hello for everyone with whom he came in contact. But now, he was so forlorn and withdrawn; as if he had aged a lifetime, in only a few short days. Jeremy had trouble recognizing him as the same man.

Since Colwyn was sorely in need of a bath and shave, he would seek them first. After that, he determined to get some rest before making much-needed inquiries in the hopes of gaining more information, before striking out again. This time he would travel towards her home himself, for he found he could no longer wait for the messenger. He vowed never to give up. For some reason, a spark of hope inside him would not die. Although from the look of things, the only conclusion he could draw was that she had chosen to leave him again.

On his way home, Colwyn did some serious thinking: *I should have found some sign by now if it were otherwise. Could she have found someone to help her? What if she intended to leave the country?* All these questions kept popping into his head and didn't want to leave until he had some answers. *Why would she let her father worry like that? Even though I had only known her a short time, I find it hard to believe her capable of something that uncaring and selfish. Surely she would have had enough courage to tell me to my face if she didn't want me.*

The cry had been sounded at his arrival, and Felicia was there, waiting to greet him in the foyer. Since her time was running out, she was beginning to get desperate. Never would she have believed Colwyn would have spent two days in the saddle looking for the little twit. That had thrown her plans awry. Frantically thinking, she decided she must slip him her potion before the end of tomorrow night and that would give her time to be the new Lady Campbell before the week was out. Then this whole ugly business of waiting could finally be put behind her.

"My God, Colwyn, you look just awful!" Felicia exclaimed at first sight of him. "Come, have a seat and rest a while." She tried to direct him to the chair but he resisted. "Have you any encouraging news?" she asked too sweetly, knowing full well that he hadn't.

The last thing Colwyn wanted to see upon arriving home was Felicia hovering over him like a mother hen. Silently he groaned to himself and almost considered turning around and going back the way he had come. But he was just too tired for that.

"No! Felicia, there is no good news, *yet,*" he emphasized the word.

"I was just going up to have a bath and shave. Would you please inform my father that I will be down in a while to speak with him? Now, if you'll excuse me."

"Colwyn, wait!" Felicia shouted as she ran in front of him at the door, so as to prevent him from walking out of the room. "Please don't leave yet. I've missed you so. Come sit with me awhile and let me pour you a drink. You must be parched."

Since Colwyn was in no mood for this, he became a little short with her as he said, "Felicia, I am not fit company for anyone just now! I'm filthy and I smell. I need a bath, but right now I must go and speak with my father. I have neither the time nor the patience to stand here and chat inanely and politely with you. I have more important matters to attend to. Go home where you belong. I'll speak with you later."

Abruptly he turned his back on her and bounded out of the room, with more energy than he felt. He decided to let the bath wait and headed for his father's study. Though he was sorry he had lost his temper with Felicia, he just couldn't deal with her clinging ways and cloying attitude at this time.

When Colwyn was gone, Felicia was left dumb-founded and at a loss for words. If she had had any true feelings, they would have been hurt. She began to tremble inside, as she realized all her carefully laid out plans were disintegrating right before her very eyes.

Colwyn rapped softly on his father's study door and waited for an answer. He knew his father was in there as he always was in there at this time of the day. Sure enough, he received a response, so he burst right in.

"Colwyn!" his father exclaimed when he looked up at his son's entrance. "Get over here and sit down! Good God! You look as if you might collapse!"

Hurrying, Colwyn did just that. Angus waited till his son was seated before he spoke again, "Damnit, boy! How could you rush out of here like that before informing me yourself what was happening?"

Colwyn tried to answer at this point but Angus didn't pause and give him time.

"And Asa, my God, son, he nearly had a heart attack when he was told!"

Angus shuddered at the memory of Asa and him in this very room, when Amy had come rushing in to tell them of Lysette's disappearance. They had been in here to celebrate the union of their families with a drink and to wait for their cue to take their places, when the ceremony began.

"He was in here with me, having a drink and toasting to your happiness. He was so looking forward to walking his daughter down the aisle, only to learn of her disappearance that way. I tell you, my breath was sucked right out of me when his color turned ashen and he keeled over. Thank God, we had the doctor here as a guest."

"I'm sorry, Father," Colwyn finally got a chance to speak, as he started to apologize for his inconsiderate behavior. "I should have told you myself, but I couldn't spare the time because I just knew if I got a quick start that I would catch up to whoever had her before they left the area

"How is Asa?" Colwyn asked, quickly changing the subject "Is he any better?"

"I'm relieved to say, he's passed the worst of his attack. The doctor has ordered him to take it easy for a while but it's hard, as he's still very anxious about his daughter. Have you not found anything?"

"No damnit!" Colwyn answered with aggravated frustration. "Not a clue."

Just as he finished saying this, Asa rushed in after hearing of Colwyn's arrival. He looked as if he had lost weight and his cheeks were sunken, but there was a glimmer of hope in his eyes as he looked about the room in the expectation of seeing his daughter.

"Colwyn, son, please tell me you've found my Lysette," he pleaded for the answer his heart desired.

"I hate to tell you this, sir, but I'm stumped. I can't find even one single clue to her whereabouts." He felt like such a failure at this moment, that he hung his head in shame.

Asa grabbed his heart and sat down, but he only seemed to be catching his breath.

"My men have been sent out to investigate also, but they haven't been able to turn up anything either," Asa started to explain.

"I don't know if I can survive this if she doesn't come home soon. I know she didn't return home to Dundee, as we've received word from the people we left behind, at Duncan castle that they haven't seen her or know anything about her whereabouts. Colwyn, you know my men are at your disposal, when next you ride out. I pray we know something soon. Forgive me, but I must leave you now," Asa continued as he began to rise from his chair with difficulty.

Colwyn reached out and helped him stand on his own two feet. "I want to pray in the chapel for her safety before retiring for the night," he ground out breathlessly but with determination.

"Colwyn, may God be with you," he told the younger man.

"May God be with you sir," Colwyn returned his blessing. "And sir, I will find her!" he added with emphasis and a certainty he felt inside.

"I hope so, young Colwyn. I hope so."

And with that, the older man left the room. Colwyn felt disheartened at his failed attempt to find something but determined not to give up. He told his father so, after Asa closed the door.

"This time, I'm going back out until I find her," his voice had the ring of an iron will.

"Colwyn, please get some rest first. Will you?" Angus urged. "You're not going to do Lysette much good if you're dead tired and collapse in the saddle."

"I know you're right," Colwyn sighed as he agreed to

the logic of his father's statement. "But I'm just so damned frustrated," he seethed through his teeth.

"You'll feel better after some sleep," Angus assured, as he patted his son on the back, much like he had done when he was a little boy.

Colwyn doubted he would get much sleep that night as he headed back up the stairs to his room.

As it turned out, his prediction came true. He kept tossing and turning, thinking he must have overlooked something that would point to the exact place where she was. Over and over he went over everything, but could come up with nothing new.

* * *

At the crack of dawn, he got up, dressed in a hurry and went down to the stables. He was eager to search the surrounding area once again and this time he intended to go by himself, as he wanted to be alone with his thoughts.

He found Jeremy already up as well and told him to saddle one of the other stallions, as he was leaving Satan behind as he had earned a much-needed rest.

Jeremy wondered why he was leaving again so soon, as he readied up Colwyn's mount. He didn't look as if he had slept a wink all night. He noticed that the young lord had changed since his lady's disappearance—it was certainly taking its toll on him. It was then that Jeremy decided to take the supply wagon nag and follow behind, in order to keep an eye on Colwyn after he set out.

It was difficult for Jeremy to keep up as Colwyn dashed across the countryside, but Jeremy was able to follow his tracks.

For some reason, Colwyn found that he was drawn back to the pond and realized that all along he had been heading straight for it. He wasn't sure just what had lured him back right now to this place. *Maybe,* he thought, *I might find a clue close by or at least some answers to my questions. But, I know it definitely had something to do with the pleasant memory he had experienced here.*

He sat on his mount at the edge of the water, just staring into the depths, picturing her face staring back up at him.

From a distance, Jeremy sat watching Colwyn. He seemed so intent on his thoughts that Jeremy knew he hadn't realized he was only a short distance away, which was strange. Almost always, Colwyn was aware of what was going on around him. That was why no one had ever got the better of him.

It was then that Jeremy finally came to the decision with what he had been struggling. *Until now, I never knew how much the beautiful young woman had meant to Lord Colwyn. To Hell with Felicia! I am proud of my newfound bravery and refuse to be frightened any longer. This is the right thing to do and I should have done so in the beginning. The information I'm about to impart will change my master back to his old self again. Also, it will make him angry, very angry, to say the least.*

Jeremy knew he had to muster up the courage and tell him now.

Colwyn heard someone approaching. He had been so lost in his thoughts; anyone could have slipped up and attacked him. Letting his guard down so easily, was reason enough for Colwyn to want to kick himself. Glancing back, he saw it was only Jeremy on the nag. A sigh of relief escaped his lips. Though he was puzzled by Jeremy's appearance, he wondered if he was needed back at the castle

"Hello, Jeremy," he called out, "what brings you here?"

"Hello, Milord," Jeremy answered back a little shy and uncertain as to how to begin. "There is something very important I need to tell you. Something I should have told you in the first place. If I had, maybe things wouldn't have got this bad."

Now Colwyn was definitely puzzled and gave the boy an odd look, but gave him his full attention, "Well, speak up, my boy. You know you can always talk to me if there's something troubling you."

"You're not going to like this," Jeremy plunged on, "but I've known what happened to her ladyship all along."

"What?" to Jeremy, Colwyn's shout seemed to echo around the world.

On the other hand, Colwyn couldn't believe his ears and asked, "How could you possibly know anything? Are you somehow involved with her disappearance and why did you wait so long to tell me this?"

Colwyn rasped out through clenched teeth, trying to keep control of the rage surging up inside him and had to remind himself that this was only a boy of eleven. Still, he couldn't help but reach out and grab Jeremy by the collar around his neck, and pull him closer to his fury. Jeremy had never seen such feral anger shooting from any human's eyes before. It was like staring into the depths of a ferocious wolf. He was mesmerized, immobile with fright.

"Answer me, boy, quickly," Colwyn's lips drew Jeremy's attention, "and you better have a damn good reason for the delay," he warned.

Jeremy decided to shoot straight to the truth.

"No milord!" he was almost crying by now. "I would never betray you by being involved in this wrong doing. I was afraid for my life, otherwise I would have told you right away. It was the Mistress Felicia, Milord, I swear. She's a witch. I seen it with my own two eyes; her and that ugly old maid of hers. They attacked Mistress Lysette out in the gardens, right afore she was to walk down the aisle to join you."

Colwyn's tight grip on Jeremy's collar seemed to loosen a little as he listened intently to the boy's explanation.

"Tell me everything you know, boy," his tone not quite so harsh now, but still commanding. "If Felicia has done anything to harm Lysette, I'll kill her!" he swore as his mind was already conjuring up an image of doing just that.

"I don't know if she's been harmed," Jeremy continued, "but they made her disappear."

Colwyn was now looking at the boy as if he'd lost his mind. "Say that again, son."

"Tis true," Jeremy uttered convincingly. "You know I wouldn't lie to you, now. She disappeared right before my eyes. I saw Miss Felicia hand milady something to drink. As she sipped from the glass, Miss Felicia started chanting in a strange language I couldn't understand. Then she threw her arms up in the air and called upon the power of the evil one."

Colwyn's face turned ashen. "All sorts of weird things began to happen then," the boy continued. "The sky began to blacken overhead and a strong wind came out of nowhere. There appeared to be lightening flashes, and when one really big one hit, it blinded me eyes. By the time I could see again, she was gone, as if she'd never even been there."

"My God!" Colwyn said, totally flabbergasted at this news. *Felicia practicing witchcraft! And why in God's name would she do such a thing? Why would she go to such lengths to harm someone who was obviously not a threat to her . . . was she?* Colwyn mused. He didn't want to dwell on that too long, however, thinking that there might be something at the back of his mind that he didn't want to remember. Then he realized that Felicia had nothing to do with God. At this point, he would put nothing past her.

"Jeremy," he said abruptly, "ride like the devil is nipping at your heels and find Mac. Tell him everything you just told me. He'll know what to do and then tell him to meet me at the Buchanan Castle.

"By God, I will know what happened to my bride-to-be in an hour's time even if I have to beat it out of the witch," were his last words to the boy.

Jeremy flicked the reigns to the horses' flank, pressed in his heels, and left a trail of dust in his wake.

9

MAC AND HIS MEN ARRIVED just as Colwyn was entering the gates of the Buchanan Castle. Colwyn could count on Mac not to waste time getting here once he learned of the situation. His man-at-arms and most trusted friend, Mac, was always there when he needed him. He was a redheaded towering hulk of a man with thick massive arms that could wrap around a man's body and crush him to death. His chest was so broad and expansive it seemed as if two men could fit inside his suit of armor. Mac's thick beard added a look of ferociousness to his bulky face; thus inspiring intimidation and fear in most of his enemies. Colwyn trusted no one but Mac with his life. But those Mac cared about knew him to be the most caring and gentlest of men.

Colwyn stormed through the doors with Mac right beside him, as the manservant answered his summons. "Where is Mistress Felicia? I must speak with her at once!" Colwyn barked out immediately.

The Buchanan's servant was a bit flustered at the unexpected arrival and Colwyn's urgent command. He was extremely curious as to what was going on, but kept his professional attitude, despite the fact that twenty men had just burst through the door looking as if they were on a death rampage.

"Why, I believe Mistress Felicia and her maid have

gone down to the dungeons again, sir," the man-servant answered Colwyn's question.

"The dungeons?" Colwyn responded, very puzzled.

"Yes sir," the servant answered with a quirk of his eyebrow. His expression clearly indicating he never questioned or tried to explain the eccentricities of his employers. Colwyn decided to let the matter drop. He didn't have time to question the man further. *But how odd,* he thought to himself. *Then again, Felicia is the oddest person I know. . . .*

He knew the dungeons were down below the kitchen area and raced there as if his feet were on fire. Mac and several others were right on his heels. As he stepped off the last step leading into the dungeon area he shouted her name so loud it sounded like thunder echoing off the walls. He waited momentarily but there was nothing but silence. "**FELICIA**!" he shouted her name again. **"Felicia! Damn-it, answer me! Where are you? It is Colwyn. I must see you immediately**!"

Through the walls of her secret room Felicia heard him and a thrill of excitement ran through her at the sound of his voice. *Good,* she thought, as a satisfied grin flashed across her face, *I will not have to seek him out again after all. He has come to me. It seems that the timing is on my side for once. He has finally come to his senses and decided to put that little bitch from his mind. He had come, she surmised, to ask me to be his bride. But he must never see the inside of this place. If he does I will lose him for sure. I know that Colwyn has a strong distaste for the practice of witchcraft.*

She knew she had to move quickly before he found out her little secret. Handing the potion she had just finished to Elsbeth, Felicia told her, "Put this in a safe place. It looks as if I won't need it now as he has come for me.

Quickly, clean up this mess!" she ordered. "I don't want to risk being exposed."

Felicia then made her way to the secret entrance and lifted the handle to exit the wall opening. As luck would have it, Colwyn was standing right next to it and he turned at the first sound he heard and burst through the entrance before Felicia had a chance to slip out. His anger was so great that at first sight of her, he wrapped his hands around her throat, cutting off her breath and lifted her feet a little in the air.

When Elsbeth witnessed what was happening, she rushed to her mistress's aid, but thought twice about it when she saw several men rush in after Colwyn. Instead, she hung back in the shadows of the room thinking, *If I crouch low in the corner behind the table maybe they won't notice me.*

"Where is she?" Colwyn shouted at Felicia's pale bulging face. "What have you done with her?"

Felicia's eyes began to water and her face began to redden from the lack of oxygen from the force he was exerting on her neck. Colwyn loosened his death grip as he watched her reaction—not out of compassion, but from rationalization. He realized he would get no answer from her if he killed her.

Coughing and sputtering, Felicia tried to recover from his abusive handling. His reaction had happened so fast her heart was about to explode from her fear. Never had she expected this reaction from him.

"Whatever are you referring to, Colwyn?" she asked, deliberately being obtuse. "I haven't the slightest idea what you are speaking about. Why are you treating me in such a manner?" she asked in a pitiful tone.

Her mind was frantically trying to think and reason:

He couldn't be talking about what I think he is. There is no way he could have found out. I will have to be most careful.

Colwyn felt nothing but disgust at her innocent act and answered, "Oh, you're good, aren't you? **I know you lie!**" he forcefully shouted the last at her. "I have a witness who saw the whole thing so I know it is you who are responsible for Lysette's disappearance!"

Her mind began racing like a squirrel in a cage and she frantically thought: *This couldn't be! I have to be dreaming. Things were not supposed to have happened this way. This was not in my plan!*

Looking into his face, she read his determination as he waited for her explanation and knew she couldn't lie her way out of this one, as she had always done so with her father. The only recourse left to her now was to try and escape, even though she knew that to be useless.

Suddenly she struggled in his grasp and kicked at his shin even though she knew her efforts were in vain as Colwyn kept a tight control of her situation. His men also were surrounded everywhere so there was no avenue of escape left open.

"Tell me now, Felicia, before I kill you on this very spot!" he shouted, very close to carrying out his threat.

Surprisingly, Felicia didn't care. She had determined she would never reveal the truth to him. That she would rather die first. Shouting her anger at Colwyn she indignantly said, "How dare you believe this falsehood you've been told? How could you take someone else's word over mine, after all we have meant to one another? After all I have given to you."

"You can stop with the theatrics now, Felicia," Colwyn answered contemptuously. "We have never meant a damn thing to one another." His words cut her like a knife and were meant to hurt. He continued, "I have never taken anything from you that you didn't freely give to me. I never gave you any promises, yet you still persisted."

"That's because I love you, Colwyn. And you love me!" Felicia declared, making one last desperate attempt to turn him around to her way of thinking. "You know this to be true, if you'd only open up your heart and examine your feelings. She's nothing, Colwyn. Nothing! Forget her and let's get on with our lives. Her measly existence doesn't matter."

"You're wrong, Felicia," Colwyn stated forcefully. "I could never love anyone as evil as you, and never say again, in my presence, that Lysette is *nothing*. She *does* matter Felicia, because I love her. Did you hear that? I love her. Now tell me what you've done with her before I choke the very life from your puny little body!" He could tell he was starting to lose control of his anger again.

"**Never**! I'll *never* tell you what happened!" Felicia shouted her defiance. "You'll have to suffer, just as you're making me suffer now."

Colwyn could take this no longer. What little bit of patience he had been holding on to had just run out and he did some quick thinking, *Leave it to Felicia to forever play the part of the one wronged instead of the wrongdoer. I estimate my best tactic to get the information I need from her would be to give her a good scare.*

His eyes did a swift scan of the surrounding area and lit on the wrist and ankle irons chained to the far stone wall for the prisoners of the keep that had to be punished. He dragged her over there, kicking and screaming all the way while his men followed closely behind. Mac had already deduced what Colwyn was up to as he saw where he was headed and grabbed one of Felicia's flaying arms and shackled it to the wall. Colwyn fastened the other. Two of his men bent quickly to confine her legs.

Meanwhile, Elsbeth watched and waited for her opportunity to escape. She had to get some help, and quickly as Colwyn looked as if he would do bodily harm to her beloved mistress, unless he got what he wanted. She saw her chance while this was all going on and everyone's back was to her. She scurried to the stairway leading back up to the kitchen, but luck was not with her now, as one of the men saw a flash out of the corner of his eye and turned to investigate. He reached her just in the nick of time.

"**Look what I found trying to sneak away like a thief in the night!**" His loud voice boomed his information to get their attention.

Colwyn turned and gestured for his man to bring her to him.

"Fasten her along side her mistress," he told him. "That is, unless she has something she would like to share with us."

"Go to hell!" Elsbeth barked at him.

"I dare say you'll be there long before I will, Madame," he quickly rejoined.

"Tell him nothing, Elsbeth. I order you," Felicia commanded her accomplice. "No matter what he does to us, don't let him scare or intimidate you."

Elsbeth took a stance and firmly closed her mouth. In the next few moments she found herself strapped beside her mistress, determined to take their secret to the grave if need be.

"Now, Felicia," Colwyn stated ominously, "I suggest you change your mind and tell me what it is I want to know before it's too late."

"You know my answer," was all she sneered.

"Do you know what they do to people accused and convicted of practicing witchcraft Felicia?" Colwyn asked her suggestively.

Felicia's eyes grew large and she gave a quick gasp as she said, "You wouldn't! You're bluffing, I know it!"

Even now, she thought to herself, *Colwyn wouldn't do anything as vile as that . . . or would he?*

"Don't be too sure, Felicia. I will do exactly that, if you don't cooperate. I have lost my last bit of patience with you, and I no longer care how you end up."

"I still don't believe you. You're only trying to scare me," Felicia stated with more confidence than she felt.

"Mac," he told his friend quite firmly. "Get prepared to start the fire. Make sure the hem of her gown catches quickly. I don't want to hear her screams for too long."

Colwyn's voice was convincingly cold and emotionless as he played his part extremely well.

Felicia still wouldn't believe he would actually go through with it so uttered not one word to obtain her freedom. Mac and a few other men gathered straw and kindling to pile around Felicia's feet.

Elsbeth looked on with horror and Colwyn then turned and addressed her by asking, "Well, are you going to let your mistress burn to death?"

Elsbeth started to speak, but with a warning look from Felicia, quickly closed her mouth.

Colwyn gave the nod to Mac to start the fire burning. Mac bent to do his bidding. Felicia looked down in disbelief as she realized he was actually going to obey Colwyn's command. He really was going to burn her to death! She took the only recourse left open to her now—she started screaming at the top of her lungs.

As soon as he had arrived home, Alexander Buchanan's manservant had informed him of Colwyn's visit to his daughter. He had also been told they were down in the dungeons. Alexander was more than a little puzzled at this news and decided he had better seek them out to find out what this business was all about.

He heard the commotion as soon as he neared the entrance to the dungeons. The ear-piercing screams made his insides curdle. Hurrying as fast as the steep steps would allow him to get there, what he saw in front of him as he arrived, nearly gave him a heart attack. Colwyn Campbell was about to have his daughter set afire.

"Colwyn, stop!" he shouted to get their attention. "What in heaven's name is going on here?" he asked as he struggled to understand the scene before him. "How can you be doing this?" he asked his young friend and neighbor with a perplexed look, very evident, in the lined wrinkles around his old and weary eyes. This just didn't make any sense at all.

Colwyn turned at Alexander's shout and motioned at Mac to step away from Felicia. "Ask your daughter, Alexander," Colwyn stated matter-of-factly, even though he felt sympathy for his long time friend, for the misery of having Felicia as his daughter. She had never considered anyone else's feelings but her own. "I'd rather you heard the truth from her so you will know of what she is capable."

Alexander turned questioning expectant eyes towards his daughter. Felicia started her tirade then, placing all the blame on Colwyn's shoulders. "You must have him arrested, father! He's lost his mind and you can't let him get away with this! He's making false accusations and threatening to kill me. I don't know what has come over him. He must be seriously ill or delusional."

"Very well then," Colwyn interrupted quite calmly, challenging the validity of her last statement. "I knew it was too much to hope to pry the truth out of you. I see I'll have to be the one to break the news to him."

He turned back towards Alexander. "Felicia is the one responsible for my fiancée's disappearance," he made the shocking statement. "She has known of her whereabouts this entire time."

"This can't be true," Alexander addressed his daughter. The worry lines etched deeper into his face. He did not want to believe this. "Felicia, tell me this isn't so. Why would Colwyn believe such a thing of you?"

"I don't know, Father," she continued to shout. "I told you, he's lost his mind."

"You are responsible, Felicia," Colwyn uttered adamantly. "Now why don't you confess and tell me where she is?"

"You've lost the power of coherent thought, Colwyn," she retaliated with contempt. "You're trying to murder an innocent woman and that is completely insane. You're the one that needs to be locked up."

"Colwyn, where is your proof?" Alexander interrupted this argument. He wanted to get to the bottom of this. "Why do you accuse my daughter of such a horrible thing? Why would you try to burn her to death?"

"I have all the proof I'll ever need," Colwyn informed him. "I have a witness who saw the whole thing. And I never would have gone through with the burning. I was only trying to scare her into confessing. I swear it, Alexander, I wouldn't have let her die that way, no matter how much I was tempted."

"I believe you, Colwyn," Alexander admitted as he continued to look at Colwyn with pain and confusion. "But you were taking an awfully drastic measure weren't you?"

"With someone as stubborn as Felicia is, it takes drastic measures," Colwyn agreed.

Alexander decided not to comment on Colwyn's last statement, as he had no defense for his daughter.

"Why do you believe this person over my daughter, Colwyn?" he asked.

"This person would never make up such a story. It involves witchcraft," Colwyn told him. "I trust that he gave me the truth. He would have no reason to lie. How could I not believe him when the evidence is apparent in this very room?" Colwyn pointed out.

Alexander really looked puzzled. He knew he had closed his eyes to Felicia's indiscretions for such a long time and wasn't sure he wanted to open them now.

"Do you really not know of your own daughter's practice of it?" Colwyn asked him. "If you don't believe me, go and look in that hidden room over there. You'll see all the articles of her wicked practices."

Alexander walked to the entrance of the hidden chamber with trepidation. Felicia watched and held her breath in anticipation. He was almost afraid to step in, afraid of what he would really find. His suspicions were proved correct as he looked about the room and surveyed the paraphernalia used in the practice of black magic. Not only was he horrified, but was also filled with deep shame, as he had always turned a blind eye to Felicia's eccentricities. Now, he had to acknowledge the fact that all of this was his fault. If he had paid more attention, he could have prevented this tragic situation. Instead, he had catered to her every whim and spoiled her atrociously and this is how she had turned out. The truth felt like a ton of bricks falling on his shoulders. He stepped back out to try and salvage what he could.

"Felicia, tell Colwyn what he wants to know!" he commanded.

Felicia couldn't believe her own ears and thought; *My own father has turned against me! This can't really be happening. He had always taken my side before. This is all Colwyn's fault.* Then she spoke up pleading, trying to turn her father back to her favor, "Father, that doesn't prove a thing. His witness is lying," she reasoned, hoping he would stop looking at her with that pitiful expression and have Colwyn and his cronies thrown out.

But, he didn't. Instead, he continued to look at his daughter hoping his next words to her would convince her to turn from her wicked ways. "I'm afraid your lies are no longer going to work, Felicia. Now, I expect the truth. You must come clean and do the right thing. Whatever you have done, I'll always be here to help you. I'm sure we can work it out together."

Felicia had never been so angry in her life at what she felt was her father's betrayal. *How could he listen to them?* "To Hell with you, Father. If you can't stand beside me on this, I want you from my sight!"

Alexander was hurt deeply by her words but knew this was the time to put an end to Felicia's corruptness. "I will *not* leave, Felicia. If you don't tell Colwyn where Lysette is, so help me God, I'll set you from this house, penniless and destitute, with nothing but the clothes on your back. Never will you be welcome here again. And I'll make sure no one in this area will ever help you. You will be cut from my family will."

How could my own father be so cruel? she wondered as she looked at his stony countenance and knew he would do exactly what he said. Felicia felt the agony of defeat but knew she still had one avenue of revenge left.

"She's far from here, Colwyn. So far away, you'll never get your hands on her," she laughed shrilly.

"What do you mean, witch?" Colwyn exclaimed. "Tell me how to get to her or you'll regret the day you were ever born! This I promise you!"

Her sadistic gleefulness sickened him to the core as she went on to explain with much pleasure, "You see, I can only call on that kind of power once. That's the deal. I'm afraid you're just out of luck!" Felicia taunted him with the reality.

"You tell me where you sent her or I will set fire to this pile. You will die right here and now with your father watching."

Colwyn now meant every word he uttered to her. He was beyond caring about her father's feelings.

"I don't know where she is. She is beyond my reach," Felicia taunted.

Actually, she had told the lie very convincingly. She knew where Lysette was as she had seen it in her crystal. She might not be able to bring her back but she knew how to do it. That was information Colwyn would never get from her.

Colwyn finally realized there was no threat he could give to Felicia to make her say one more thing. He would never get the full truth out of her. But he wouldn't give up hope now. Somewhere there was someone who could help him. He just had to find him. For now, though, he could no longer stand the sight of this witch or this stinking place. He had to be gone from this place and start seeking.

"Goodbye, Alexander." Colwyn offered his farewells to his friend, as he bore no ill will towards him. "I must be on my way. You're welcome to her but I know of no one who envies you."

He turned to leave but Alexander had something to

tell him. "Colwyn, wait!" he urged. "I think I know of someone who may be able to help you."

"Tell me, who is it?"

Colwyn became excited and hopeful again at Alexander's disclosure. "On one of my business trips to the highlands of Inverness," Alexander began his tale, "I heard tell of a man who goes by the name of Ian Douglas. They say he's a seer of some sort, and really quite amazing.

"It seems he helped a very distraught young couple find their lost little son. They had just about given up all hope of ever finding him alive. The search had been going on for days but nothing had been turned up. That is, until someone advised them to ask this man for help.

"A few days earlier, a group of friends had been playing a game of hide and seek in the woods. This young boy went further off, on his own, quite a bit further than he was supposed to go. No one had seemed to notice in which direction he had taken off. When it was time to come in, he couldn't be found. A search party was formed in the town but they couldn't get any answers as they scoured about the area. It was beginning to look pretty grim.

"Then, this Ian Douglas was asked to help. They say he mostly keeps to himself, rather a hermit, but he agreed to it. Hear tell it, the power came to him after he suffered an accident. Lightening struck him full force and he survived. Afterwards, he would see things that he couldn't explain. Visions they call 'em. They get stronger whenever he happens to be handling an object or a prized possession of the person who owns it. Most people were afraid of him and had him ostracized from the town. But this young couple was desperate."

"They gave him one of the boy's favorite toys he had played with recently. Ian saw him in one of his visions. He had fallen into a boar trap three miles up from where the children were playing. When he had tripped, he had fallen on a rock, hit his head and knocked himself out. For the next few days he lay unconscious. That's how Ian saw him and he told them where to find him.

"The town folk had never figured he could have wandered off that far. Fortunately, the boy wasn't seriously hurt and quickly recovered from his coma. I met both him and his parents in Inverness and spoke with them. They seemed totally convinced of Ian Douglas' authenticity and were eternally grateful for his help. They did a complete turn around in their thinking about the power he possessed."

Hope was again renewed in Colwyn after hearing Alexander's story. "Thank you, Alexander." He went to shake his friend's hand and said, "You can't imagine the gratitude I feel towards you for sharing this information with me."

Alexander was slightly embarrassed at the situation and replied, "It's the least I could do after the trouble my daughter has caused you."

"You know I don't blame you," Colwyn assured him. "But I must get going now. I have quite a ways to travel."

"Colwyn, when you get there, ask for the innkeeper at the Inverness Inn. He'll know where you can find Ian Douglas," Alexander offered this last bit of helpful information.

Felicia had watched the exchange between her father and Colwyn with disgust. She would never forgive her father for helping him now. But she couldn't resist one last dig at Colwyn's retreating back and she retorted with spite, "I wouldn't get my hopes up too high, Colwyn. Even if you do find her, she won't remember who you are. You see, I gave her a potion that would do away with her memory."

Colwyn turned and stared at her smirking face, feeling a desperate urge to wrap his powerful hands around her throat and strangle the life out of her. Instead, he came to the conclusion she wasn't worth the effort or the time it would take. As far as Lysette's memory loss, he would just have to deal with that once he had found her. There was no question in his mind, whatsoever, that he would find her. He would search until every avenue had been explored and then some!

"May you rot in hell, Felicia!" was his parting remark to her before he vanished from sight.

Alexander quickly unlocked his daughter and her maid from their shackles. When he tried to help his daughter up the stairs, she would have none of him. Alexander felt sick at heart at her rejection and vowed to make it up to her. Right now, she was not in a forgiving mood, but Alexander felt sure she would soon come around.

* * *

At the stroke of midnight, Felicia sat bolt upright in bed, awakened from a horrifying dream. The room seemed consumed by a suffocating heat causing Felicia to feel as if she was melting. She immediately sensed she was not alone in the room.

"Who's there?" she cried out in fright.

"I've come to collect on the debt owed," the voice of doom whispered in the darkness.

The next morning, a piercing scream of anguish ripped the air as it reached to the farthest corners of every wing in the castle. Elsbeth had just entered Felicia's bed-chamber to help with her morning toilet. As she pulled back the covers to wake her precious sleepy-head, she found nothing but a pile of molten bones and ashes.

10

Summer, 2005

Edinburgh, Scotland

LYSETTE WAS CONFUSED AND ALLOWED the young woman to lead her to a nearby park bench. "Would you like to sit down for a little while and catch your breath?" she asked her.

Lysette looked at the woman oddly and just nodded in response.

"You look as pale as a ghost right now. Is there anything I can get you?" the young woman kindly asked. She was becoming more than a little concerned at this young woman's state of shock.

In a state of wonder, Lysette gazed about her. She had never been to a place such as this and nothing about it seemed familiar.

"May I have something to drink, please?" Lysette asked the stranger.

"Sure, I'll bring you some tea and be right back. You just wait right here. It won't take but a minute," the young woman told her before she hurried over to a picnic table.

While she was gone, Lysette had a chance to observe the people and her surroundings. She had to ask herself, *Where is this place and how did I get here?* The more she looked, the more convinced she became that she had stumbled into a society of witches. There were things going on here that couldn't be possible without the power of magic. Everyone was dressed in a strange manner, objects were traveling at speeds unheard of, and even sounds were coming out of little black boxes the young people were carrying around. *Yet the young woman had seemed so kind. How could she be a witch? Was this all a ruse to trick me?*

Lysette had decided she had better not stick around and find out and jumped up to run as fast as her shaky legs would allow her. The young woman saw her as she glanced her way and dropped the tea she was carrying back to Lysette. She caught up to her in no time.

"Whoa, hold on a minute," she said as she reached out and caught her. "What's the matter? You act as if you're scared out of your wits and running for your life."

Lysette had no choice but to stop. In her weakened state, she knew struggling would be useless. "What are you going to do to me?" Lysette burst out. "Are you all witches? How did I come to be in your coven?"

The woman's mouth dropped open in surprise. She was so surprised she let go of Lysette all together. "What in the world are you talking about?" she exclaimed. "Wherever did you get an idea like that?"

Lysette looked at her companion's surprised face and asked rather uncertainly, "You mean you're not a witch?"

"Of course not," the lady answered. "No one here would ever hurt you. Now come sit back down and let's talk about what happened to you and why you would think that."

She led Lysette back to the bench then continued, "Let's just take a moment to relax and then you can tell me who you are and how you came to be here"

"You mean you don't know how I got here?" Lysette asked her in wonder.

"Me!" the young woman mouthed astonished. "How would I know? First you weren't here, and then all of the sudden, you seemed to appear as if out of nowhere. I looked up, from setting some food on the table, and there you were. You mean you don't remember how you got here?" the young woman gasped in surprise. She was at a loss now, and wasn't sure how to deal with this situation.

"Well, how about your name?" she thought to ask at last. "Do you at least know that?"

"I can't seem to remember anything just now," Lysette sounded a little disoriented. "What is the name of this place? I don't recognize anything about this area."

"Why, this is Edinburgh, Scotland," the stranger answered, "and we're in the park across the street from the First Presbyterian Church."

Lysette's expression indicated she was still at a loss, as what she had said had no meaning for her.

"Don't fret now," the woman tried to reassure her by patting Lysette's hand with her own. "You know, I read somewhere that for the most part, memory loss is only temporary. I'm sure it will return shortly. Anyway, whoever you are, it looks as if you were about to be married. I don't see a wedding band on your finger, so I'm guessing that you didn't go through with it."

Lysette glanced down at the breathtaking creation in which she was dressed and her left hand, but still no memory came to her. She just drew a blank.

"By the way, I'm Lorna Tompkins," the woman broke the silence that settled between them, "and I'm very glad to meet you."

After introducing herself, she held out her hand to shake Lysette's. "Sorry about my tardy introduction, but you had me going for a bit," she smiled at this statement, trying to put Lysette more at ease.

Lysette took her offered hand with a slight hesitation and made her apologies as well. "I'm sorry that I accused you earlier of being a witch, but I was, and still am, really confused. I wish I could tell you my name but I just can't seem to remember it at the moment."

"Don't worry, I'm sure you soon will be able to," Lorna tried to speak with confidence.

Lysette decided she liked this attractive young woman with the mid-length, brunette hair that she wore down and free-swinging, aqua-blue eyes and a most friendly smile. It was this last feature she possessed that convinced Lysette to trust her.

"Now let's get to this business of why you thought we were witches," Lorna encouraged her to speak.

"Well, your manner of dress and speech for one thing," Lysette told her.

It was Lorna's turn now to look confused as she continued to listen.

"And your mode of travel," Lysette continued. "How can anything go that fast, especially without horses? And what are those?" she indicated as she pointed to the young man that was toting the boom box on his shoulder. "There are voices and sounds that seem to be coming from them and these things could not be possible without some kind of magic."

Lorna's confusion was still quite evident as Lysette saw it written all over her face. She was at a loss as to which subject to tackle first, so decided to go with the easiest and start with her clothes.

"What's so strange about my dress?" she asked.

"It's highly indecent," Lysette informed her hotly.

Lorna was wearing a form-fitting tangerine dress

that to Lysette appeared to be a slip that was too tight. On her feet, she wore a pair of leather thong sandals.

"Indecent!" Lorna shouted this. "I'll have you know this is a Calvin Klein," she uttered proudly, with a downward swoosh of her arm. "It set me back a whole paycheck."

Lysette stared at Lorna because the words she had uttered had no meaning to her. *Who is Calvin Klein and what is a paycheck?* Lysette wondered to herself. She refrained from saying anything though, as Lorna continued.

"If you're referring to the vehicles that move without the aid of horses, they are called cars. They have gas-powered engines that run them. Nobody uses a horse, except for pleasure and recreation. And the voices coming out of the little black boxes are called boom boxes and the teenagers around here listen to the music from the radio stations or from cassettes and CDs that they pop in and play."

Lysette still had no idea what she was talking about and Lorna could see that and asked her, "How is it that you don't know of these things?"

She looked at Lysette as if she'd stepped from another world and said, "It sounds as if you came from the Middle Ages." This she had said in a joking manner, never suspecting how close to the truth she had come.

But Lysette took her question seriously and said, "I truly don't remember any of these things you've just described. Nothing seems as it should be. I don't think or feel that I belong here."

Lorna began to get a little worried now and asked, "Have you injured yourself? Did you hit your head, and are you in pain anywhere? Sometimes a head injury can cause more damage than we suspect."

“I don’t think so,” Lysette responded slowly as she assessed her body. “I don’t feel any pain.”

“Let me examine your head to feel if there are any bumps,” Lorna told her. “I want to make sure so as to be on the safe side.”

“Okay, if you say so.”

Lysette sat patiently as Lorna felt all over her head, even though she felt ill at ease by this attention.

“Well, I don’t feel anything. And I’m sure if you had any fresh bruises, the skin would still be tender.”

Lorna looked up then as she finished checking over Lysette and saw her mother and the Reverend Morgan walking their way.

“That’s my mom and the reverend coming this way, now,” she happily exclaimed to Lysette. “Maybe they have some ideas as to how we can help you.

“Mom, Reverend Morgan,” she called out to them, “over here. I have something I wish to discuss with you.”

Lorna’s mother and the reverend joined them a few seconds later as they quickened their pace at her call.

“Hello, dear,” Lorna’s mother addressed her. “What do you want to tell me and who is this beautiful young lady with you?” she asked politely, even though her curiosity was working hard to get the best of her.

“It is *she* who we need to talk about, Mom,” Lorna told her. “This young lady desperately needs our help. She seems to have appeared out of nowhere but has lost her memory; but she assures me she hasn’t been injured.”

“Oh, my goodness!” the elder woman exclaimed. “How awful for you, my dear. My name is Martha Tompkins and this is the Reverend Morgan. He is pastor here at the First Presbyterian Church,” she made the introductions to Lysette. “How can we help you?”

"I'm not really sure," Lysette answered. "I feel strange."

"Do you feel ill?" the reverend piped in with concern.

"Not really," she answered. "Just overwhelmed with my memory loss."

"We should still have you taken to a professional to be examined, even if you feel you haven't been injured, just to make certain. I've heard of temporary memory losses resulting from very traumatic experiences. Yours could be trauma related. In any case, I have a friend who is a specialist in that area. His name is Dr. Warner and he is also a member of our church. Martha, I believe you've met him," Reverend Morgan stated.

"Yes, of course," Mrs. Tompkins remarked. "I like him tremendously."

"Unfortunately, he is not here with us today," the reverend informed them. "However, his office is only a few miles away from here." The reverend continued, "I'll call him at home and ask him to meet you there. I'm sure he'd be happy to do so."

Then he turned to Lorna and said, "His office is on the top floor of the hospital. You should be able to find it easily enough."

"Yes, I believe I can," Lorna responded.

"Will you drive this young lady there while I make the call and apprise the doctor of the situation?" the reverend asked her.

"Certainly, I'll do so," she readily agreed.

She then turned back to Lysette after the reverend had finished speaking and kindly asked, "Would you like to come with me and my mom to see if we can get you some help?"

Lysette really couldn't explain why, maybe it was just the kindness they were showing her, but she decided she could trust these strange people. Their concern came across as genuine, even though they were strangers in a very unbelievable atmosphere.

"Yes, I will go with you," Lysette answered with confidence.

"Good," Lorna replied. "Let's get going then."

Lorna led her to an ice blue colored Mazda Miata parked in the church parking lot. When Lysette realized where they were headed, she pulled back from them. Lorna immediately picked up on her reservations and assured her, "It's alright. I got my license from the bottom of a cracker-jack box." She laughed at her own joke trying to put Lysette's mind at ease. That is until she realized Lysette didn't quite get it and was genuinely frightened of the strange vehicle.

"Really, it's alright. I'm an excellent driver, even if I do say so myself," Lorna assured her.

"I'll tell you what. I'll go very slowly if that will make you feel better. I promise I won't do anything to frighten you."

Lysette's reservations seemed to ease some at Lorna's reassuring tone, and allowed them to help her into the front passenger seat

Reverend Morgan was there beside them before going into the church to make his call to the doctor. He said to Lorna before she pulled out, "I'm also going to make some calls to the neighboring churches to inquire if they know anything about this young lady's disappearance."

"That's a good idea," Lorna remarked. "I'm sure we'll be able to find something out by tonight. We'll meet you back here after the doctor examines her."

"Good, I'll be waiting for you. You ladies have a safe trip and may God be with you. See you in a little while," Reverend Morgan said with an encouraging smile.

"Thank you, Reverend. Bye now," Lorna waved as she drove away.

As they were heading towards their destination, Lorna tried to cover up the awkward silence by voicing her thoughts out loud. "You know, I've been thinking," she said to Lysette. "Maybe you come from a community much like the Amish in Pennsylvania. They shun everything that is modern. That might explain why you don't seem to know about cars and paved roads and even the clothes you consider indecent."

"I really wish I could remember," Lysette sighed in despair.

"We'll check that possibility out," Lorna informed her, "just in case we don't find out anything by tonight."

"Wait a minute," Martha Tompkins piped up from the back seat. "You didn't say anything before about her not remembering anything modern."

"I'll explain later, Mom," Lorna told her. "Right now let's find out what the doctor can tell us."

Lysette was amazed at how fast the trip lasted as she heard Lorna exclaim, "We're here," just as they arrived pulling into the hospital parking lot.

She had just begun enjoying her first car ride and looking at all the fascinating scenery after her nervousness had abated when Lorna led her into an enormously tall, magnificent building. Lysette was immediately struck by the sterile smell of the place and she wrinkled her nose.

Lorna directed her to the admitting and information desk and spoke to the woman there. Lysette remained silent during this whole exchange trying to take in all the unfamiliar surroundings.

Next came the elevator with the doors that opened by *themselves*. Lysette certainly didn't want to step into that. She resisted by stepping back. Again, Lorna urged her on by convincing her of the safeness but Lysette was still wary of such a contraption and could not see the point of such an endeavor. In the end, though, she complied, standing beside Lorna as she pushed some circles on the wall and the doors closed. When the floored moved, Lysette grabbed Lorna's arm with a vice-like grip and nearly passed out from the shock. But patiently, Lorna held her firmly and uttered comforting words to help her keep her consciousness. Just the same, Lysette was immensely relieved when the contraption finally stopped, the doors opened and she was able to step back out onto stable ground.

Thanks to the reverend's call, Dr. Warner was expecting them and ushered them right in. He was a distinguished looking gentleman in his fifties with only a slight touch of gray highlighting his still dark hair. He had smiling blue eyes and an encompassing warmth that seemed to put a person at ease right away. On first sight, Lysette decided she liked him and hoped he could tell her something that would help her.

Lorna asked to speak with him alone a minute, while her mother and Lysette waited in the waiting room. As soon as the door was closed behind them, Lorna launched right into her litany. "Dr. Warner," she began, "there is something about her case I feel you must know. She claims she has no physical injuries and we have found no evidence of any, but she can't remember a thing about herself. Not only that, she doesn't seem to remember anything of the modern world. It's as if she has been completely cut off from society. Also, she's never even seen an automobile or a paved road for that matter. She thinks we should still be riding around in horse-drawn carts, that we speak atrociously, dress indecently and that we all come from a coven of witches."

Dr. Warner's eyes widened in unbelievable surprise at the information Lorna had just imparted to him. In all his years of practice, he had never been up against a case such as this.

"This is the most extraordinary thing I've ever come across," he admitted to Lorna. "I've counseled amnesia patients extensively, but always before, they couldn't remember anything pertaining to themselves, but normal everyday life matters were still commonplace. Maybe she comes from a society that shuns everyday modern conveniences."

"That's exactly what I thought," Lorna told him excitably. "Like the Amish people perhaps?"

"Perhaps," the doctor tried to sound introspective. "I'll have to interview her to see if I can gain some insight as to what led up to her memory loss. But first, she needs a physical exam. We have to find out if her condition could be medically related. Every possible cause must be explored and ruled out before proceeding to the next step. Will you have her step in here now, please, so I may speak with her?" he asked Lorna.

"Certainly, I'll go get her," Lorna responded as she reached for the door handle.

Just a few short seconds went by and Mrs. Tompkins and Lorna entered his office with her new charge on her arm.

"Hello again, young lady," Dr. Warner boomed his welcome. "Won't you please take a seat?"

Lysette sat down in the chair he indicated.

"Would you be more at ease if your companion stayed with you while we talk for awhile?"

"Yes, I would like that very much," Lysette sighed with relief.

She hadn't known these ladies very long, but still they were the most familiar people in this place. Lorna and Mrs. Tompkins took a seat behind Lysette, yet close enough to lend their comforting support.

"Now," Dr. Warner began by saying, "you claim you believe you have not been injured in any way. Is that correct?" Dr. Warner waited for her response.

"Yes," she answered quickly. "I believe that is so, for I don't feel any pain or discomfort anywhere."

"We'll need to do a complete physical examination just to be on the safe side," he told her. "I'll also have to run a few tests. Now, I don't want you to be frightened. I'll only be trying to find out a little more about your medical health. You shouldn't feel much pain from these tests, but you may feel a little. If you'd so like, your lady friends may stay with you the whole time, if that would make you feel more comfortable."

"Thank you," Lysette spoke up, "I'd like that."

Just then, the phone shrilled loudly by her ear and Lysette jumped in surprise. "What is that?" she exclaimed.

Lorna responded quickly. "That's just the telephone ringing," she explained to Lysette as she calmed her by placing her hands reassuringly on her shoulders. "The phone is what we use as a tool for communicating with other people. You needn't be frightened. I promise it was not created by witchcraft."

Dr. Warner had gone ahead and answered it, but was completely aware of the exchange between the two women.

"You see," Lorna went on to explain, "the doctor is

speaking into the mouthpiece and the person on the other end can hear what he is saying."

Lysette looked at her as if she had lost her mind, but found herself curious about the possibility. The doctor leaned over and let her listen into the receiver while the caller was speaking. Lysette's mouth dropped open in amazement.

As Dr. Warner ended his conversation, he felt he had a lot to unlock in his young patient's mind.

"Come on then, young lady. Let's go see if we can find out what's ticking away in that brain of yours."

Lysette found herself more perplexed than before, at the doctor's comment.

11

DR. WARNER EXPLAINED, STEP BY step, the purpose of each test. He was patient and understanding of her reservations while he chatted in a friendly but stick-to-the-issues manner. His conversation didn't mean much to Lysette, but at least it distracted her a little from the uneasiness. Lorna and her mother were also an added comfort. Everything went along smoothly, that is, until they came to the CAT scan room.

The monstrosity looked far too large and forbidding to use on humans and, even though they explained the procedure to her in detail, she didn't really understand how they expected anyone to calmly glide into that thing without putting up a fight. In the first place, the idea of being strapped down and unable to move panicked her to no end. Secondly, it appeared that once underway the thing would swallow her whole, no questions asked.

Patiently Dr. Warner tried to explain to her, "A CAT scan is an advanced system for medical X-ray imaging of the interior of the body. It provides images that give much more detailed information than ordinary X-ray pictures."

Lysette was thinking: *Since I don't even know what an X-ray is in the first place, how does he think more information is going to help me better understand what they want me to do?*

Noticing Lysette's reluctance, Lorna decided to lend her assistance.

"Hey, look," she confessed to Lysette, "I had one done a couple of years back and it didn't hurt a bit. You see, with this new kind of technology they can find out all sorts of things about what is going on inside a person's head. If perhaps it should turn out to be serious, then the doctor has a better chance of finding the problem earlier and hopefully able to treat it more effectively. Please trust me, Lysette. It will be okay, you'll see. I'll be right here the whole time and won't leave your side," she promised.

Lysette calmed down somewhat after Lorna's assurances and agreed to allow the procedure to begin. Amazingly, it was over within a relatively short time and she was pleasantly surprised to find that Lorna had been correct—it hadn't hurt at all.

There was one thing that still puzzled her and that was why they had named the "monster" after a cat. Upon voicing her question, they all had had a good laugh while Lysette only looked more perplexed. When Lorna was able to recover sufficiently, she wiped her eyes, gave a little giggle then did her best to explain. "The word *CAT* is an acronym for Computerized Axial Tomagraphy."

In great detail, Lorna tried her best to explain, but poor Lysette felt she didn't know any more than she had before.

Dr. Warner then announced to everyone, "I should have the results of Lysette's tests by tomorrow morning or at the latest, in the afternoon. In any case, young lady, I will call you tomorrow and let you know the results. Where can I reach you?" he asked Lysette.

Lorna quickly piped up and said, "She will be staying with me." Lysette gave her a grateful look while Lorna wrote down her telephone number.

* * *

They all left Dr. Warner's office shortly after that and headed back to the church to see if the reverend had found out anything yet. When they arrived the reverend had disappointing news waiting for them. No other churches in the area had a wedding scheduled for that day and no one was missing a bride. He did impart some good advice though by suggesting they go to the local police station where it was just possible somebody might have reported her missing by then.

Thanking the reverend for all his help they soon left for Lorna's house.

After only a few short minutes on the road again, Lorna heard Lysette's stomach rumble. Though Lysette was a little embarrassed by the noise her stomach loudly emitted, Lorna's reaction was to instantly be apologetic at her oversight.

"Oh, my God, you must be starving!" she exclaimed to Lysette. "I'm so sorry I didn't offer you something to eat before now. We'll get something right away," she told her spotting a McDonald's up ahead. "The visit to the police station can wait a few more minutes. Do you like hamburgers?" Lorna asked.

"I don't know," Lysette answered. "What's a hamburger?"

"You've never eaten a hamburger before?" Lorna replied incredulously. "Well, you're in for a treat. Do you mind if we go through the drive-thru and eat in the car? I'm afraid in a fast food restaurant you'd stick out like a sore thumb in that wedding dress."

"No, I don't mind," Lysette responded. Truth be told, she only agreed because she had not a clue what Lorna meant by a "drive-thru" or "fast food restaurant."

At the drive-thru kiosk, Lorna ordered a Big Mac, large fries, and a large coke for each of them. When Lysette took her first bite of the hamburger, she instantly decided she liked it very much. The fries weren't bad either; especially when she followed Lorna's example and dipped them in a red sauce called ketchup. However, she reserved her opinion about the coke, as she couldn't decide whether or not she liked the bubbles tickling her nose. She thought it might be a taste one had to acquire over time.

Being starved, it seemed Lysette devoured her meal in no time and was just finishing her last bite when Lorna drove into the police station's parking lot.

Inside the police station was an eye-opener for Lysette. It was a beehive of activity filled with many interesting, yet strange, types of people. With so much noise coming from several people in front of them crying for attention, Lysette couldn't help but wonder if anybody would even notice them.

She remembered Lorna telling her that if anybody had reported her missing, even if from another precinct, the police would be able to tell her in only a matter of minutes.

When their turn finally came at the front of the desk, Sgt. Harold McVie stood behind waiting to hear their request. He seemed pleasant, but more than a little distracted by the ringing of his phone. Asking them to please wait a moment, he shortly finished his conversation then turned his attention to them.

"What can I do to help you ladies this evening?" he asked.

Lorna explained Lysette's situation and asked him, "By any chance has anyone reported her as a missing person?"

He replied, "Give me a minute and I will check through the computer to see if anyone answering her description has been listed."

After a few moments he informed them, "No one has come in here to report her missing. In fact, we have not received any missing person reports today." Then he added, "Usually a person isn't considered missing until twenty-four hours has passed—unless, of course, there are special circumstances that apply."

Both young women felt that Lysette's memory loss made her case positively applicable.

Going back to the computer, Sgt. McVie continued to check with the other precincts. The news he gave them was not very encouraging. "No one fitting your description has been reported missing in any of the surrounding areas. But if anyone does I will need a name, address and telephone number where we can get in touch with her."

Lorna told the sergeant Lysette would be staying with her so gave him her information. She also gave him her work number in case he couldn't reach Lysette at her home.

Then Sgt. McVie suggested, "Let's take Lysette's picture in order for it to be faxed to the other local precincts so they could also be on the lookout for anyone trying to find her."

Obviously puzzled, Lysette agreed after Lorna explained what the police sergeant meant and why the proposed procedure was a good idea.

"Please step behind the line on the floor," the sergeant requested. After Lysette did so, he pointed a small black box in her direction and then there was a flash of light that momentarily blinded her. Suspecting this was Lysette's first time at getting her picture taken, Lorna was right there, reassuring her that her sight would return to normal in just a few seconds.

When the desk sergeant showed the young ladies the final result, Lysette was absolutely speechless and told herself, *It must be some type of magic trick that can reproduce one's image on a piece of white stuff called computer paper.*

Before Lorna and Lysette left, Sgt. McVie offered them one last suggestion: "Make several flyers with her photo on it and post it around the local spots in case somebody sees it and recognizes her."

They thanked him profusely for all his help and he modestly responded, "It was no problem as I'm sure not likely to forget her. Never before has anybody come in here asking for help in such a charming wedding gown. It was such a pleasant change from the usual crowd of overly tattooed, body pierced, pink and purple-haired weirdos we usually have to deal with."

As they were heading back to Lorna's car, Lysette confessed to Lorna, "I'm beginning to feel a little self-conscious and uncomfortably hot in this gown."

Lorna told her, "Now don't you worry. I'll take you back to the apartment I share with my roommates. They won't mind at all. In fact, they'd love to help. First we'll get you into a nice hot bath and then it's straight to bed for you, young lady. The trauma of this day has taken its toll on you more than you realize and you need the rest. In the morning you can borrow some of my clothes. That is, after I drop Mom off at her house."

Though Lysette appreciated all Lorna's kindness and help, the nice hot bath sounded like the most wonderful thing in the world. Then the thought of slipping between cool sheets, on a soft comfy bed, put a relaxed smile on her face for the first time that night. But she had to admit she'd have to think twice about borrowing any clothes from Lorna if what her new friend was wearing now was any indication of everything she owned.

* * *

They arrived at Lorna's apartment shortly after they left Mrs. Tompkins off at her home. Upon entering, Lorna asked Lysette to take a seat on the couch while she went in search of her roommates.

Still standing, Lysette looked around the room and thought it was quite charming even though it contained some strange items she couldn't identify. Upon sitting down on the sofa she was somewhat surprised at how comfortable it was. She hoped Lorna would hurry back soon because she was so tired she was afraid that upon finally returning she would find her new friend dead asleep on the soft couch. Already Lysette was vaguely aware she was beginning to relax and her eyes were heavy as though weights were attached, forcing them to close.

Lorna found her two roomies in Susan's room where they were diligently helping her study for the Bar Exam. It took Lorna only a matter of minutes to relate Lysette's unfortunate situation and as she expected, they were immediately sympathetic. They assured her they would be glad to help Lysette in any way they could and that it would not be any imposition at all for her to stay with them for a while.

"Thanks, guys," Lorna smiled her gratitude. "I knew I could count on you. Come, I'd like you to meet her. I left her in the living room while I went to find you."

The two roomies followed Lorna. Upon entering the living room with her two, very attractive roomies in tow, they startled Lysette who jumped at the sound of their arrival as she had just dozed off.

Understanding, Lorna went to her and began the introductions. "This is Stacy Reynolds," she told Lysette; indicating a statuesque, green-eyed blonde.

"Hello, I'm very glad to meet you," Stacy said as she went forward to shake Lysette's hand. "And you are very welcome to stay here as long as you need," she added with a smile.

Lysette shook the woman's hand and offered her gratitude. "Thank you," she uttered. "You are most kind."

"No problem," the blonde waved off her gratitude. "We're glad to do it."

Lysette noticed they seemed to say the phrase, "No problem" quite often. It was one of their many odd peculiarities of speech she had heard that day.

"And this," Lorna continued, after Stacy and Lysette's exchange, "is Susan Howard." She indicated the rather diminutive blue-eyed redhead.

The second roomy was also just as friendly. As she reached for Lysette's hand Susan gave her a big smile and told her, "That goes ditto for me."

Though Lysette shook Susan's hand readily enough, she found herself puzzling in bewilderment at what the word "ditto" meant.

"Welcome to our home," the three echoed in unison.

"We all work at Kent & Hennessey," Lorna informed Lysette. "It's a law firm. Stacy was helping Susan study for the Bar Exam when I found them in Susan's room. She wants to become a lawyer herself instead of working for one."

The three roomies laughed at their own private joke while Lysette just stood there looking perplexed. Most of what they had just said had confused her even more and she could feel the beginnings of a headache.

As soon as their laughter faded Lysette asked with awe, “You mean women can become lawyers?”

“Why yes, of course,” Susan answered. “Women have been lawyers for ages now and also doctors or anything they want to be for that matter.”

Lysette still had a look of disbelief on her face and noticing this, Susan drew Lorna aside so no one could overhear their conversation.

“Lorna,” she whispered, “I know you said she had lost her memory but this is bad! How could she not know about women doctors and lawyers?”

Lorna just shrugged her shoulders and as she slightly shifted her eyes whispered, “I’ll explain it all a little later after she goes to bed.”

Susan just nodded her head, not really knowing what to think of Lysette at that point.

“I wish I could remember at least *something,*” Lysette uttered her distress. “Even if it is only a small thing. Maybe then I could better understand why *nothing* seems familiar to me.” Just then a new thought occurred to her: “I know we’re in Edinburgh, Scotland, as Lorna already informed me,” she announced, “but I can’t recall what year it is.”

“Why—it’s the year 2005,” Stacy answered. Does that mean anything to you, or ring any bells?” she then asked Lysette.

“I have a feeling the year should mean something very important to me,” Lysette said as she momentarily reflected on her innermost thoughts. “But I can’t think why. Down deep inside of me I don’t feel as if I really belong here. There is something that is not right about this—”

Lorna interrupted her then before she became too tense and worried about her situation saying; "Don't try to think too hard on it now as you'll only give yourself a headache. What you need now is a good rest. I'd be willing to bet it'll all come back—though probably a little at a time."

Right then all Lysette could do was hope. Stacy chose that moment to speak again saying, "You know, guys, I just thought of something. We have to come up with a name to call her. We can't just go around calling her 'Hey, you!' every time we want her attention."

"You're right about that," Lorna added. Then turning to Lysette she asked, "Is there a name you're particularly fond of that we can call you?"

"I don't know," Lysette pondered. "I haven't really thought of that before."

Susan decided to put her two-cent's worth in by saying, "In that case, do you mind if I choose a name for you?"

With a little smile Lysette nodded her agreement.

"I've always been fond of the name Lisa myself," Susan announced. "Would you have any objections to being referred to as Lisa?"

Upon a moment's reflection Lysette said, "Why, no. I like the sound of it too. It seems fitting somehow and almost familiar."

Evidently, the name Lisa struck some cord in her memory.

"Good," they all three chorused together, breaking Lysette's concentration.

"Lisa it is then, until your memory returns," announced Lorna.

Lysette smiled then and felt very moved by their kindness to her. She was very much in danger of becoming over-emotional so in order to dam up and prevent the tears from flowing, she spoke up saying, "You three have been most kind. I don't think I could ever do enough to repay you."

"No problem," they all spoke as one.

There is that same phrase again, Lysette told herself. *I know that if I was with these girls for any length of time I would soon pick up their vocabulary habits.*

"Right now, I'd like a cup of hot tea. How about you ladies?" Lorna asked.

"Oh yes, that sounds heavenly," Susan answered while the other two just nodded in agreement.

"But first, Lisa," Lorna tried out Lysette's new name. "I'm going to run you a hot bath. You can borrow one of my nighties for bed since we're both about the same size. After that, we'll have our tea before turning in. You can sleep in my bed tonight," she told Lysette. "I'll sleep on the couch."

"Oh, no!" Lysette exclaimed. "I don't want to put you out of your own bed."

"Don't think a thing about it. I don't mind at all." Lorna went on to explain, "The couch is quite comfy because it has a sleeper mattress inside."

Lysette had a look of utter amazement on her face. Listening to the girls they made her feel as if anything was possible.

"Besides," Lorna continued, "I want you to have an undisturbed night's rest. Maybe by then some part of your memory might return."

Lysette just smiled agreeably as she realized she would not win any arguments this night. Besides, she hoped Lorna was right and she would regain her memory by morning.

A few minutes later, Lysette's eyes got as round as saucers when she watched running water flow into the tub in the small, but attractively decorated bathroom. To her it seemed that life here was very convenient.

Seeing that Lysette was not familiar with the concept of the bathroom/running water, Lorna explained all about bathrooms and indoor plumbing. Lysette listened and was flabbergasted. Later, as she soaked in the luxuriously scented bath water, she still found herself wondering why she couldn't remember a lifestyle with so much ease.

After her bath, the four ladies joined up again in the kitchen and had their tea. Stacy suggested, as they were finishing up: "Well, it's off to bed for me to get a good night's rest. I suggest the three of you do the same. In the morning I have to go to work and you know what a grouch I can be when I haven't had a sufficient amount of beauty sleep."

Lorna and Susan both burst into a rousing bout of laughter at Stacy's statement.

"That's quite enough, you two," she admonished with a grin. Surprisingly this response seemed to make the roomies laugh all the harder. Lysette sat there puzzling over their strange behavior, wondering what to make of the three young ladies.

Despite Lorna's wishes that Lysette should get some much-needed sleep, she spent a very restless night. She kept waking up from a recurring dream that made her feel quite flushed. In the dream she was standing by a pond in the countryside somewhere. It was very peaceful and beautiful. An unmistakable feeling came over her that she never wanted to leave that place while at the same time, she also began to feel a little anxious and excited, though she didn't understand why.

Then *he* was there; looking down at her with a desire that thrilled her down to her very toes. He was the most attractive man she could ever recall seeing. Instinctively she realized she must know him. His emerald eyes held hers and his powerfully built arms slowly wrapped around hers, drawing her down to the soft, mossy earth. Not knowing how, she realized she was suddenly without any clothes. It was as if they had disappeared in a blink of an eye.

His touch made her feel things she had never known existed. Her insides became as molten fire and she felt the two of them were melting together. There was a tingling sensation in her lower pelvic region and she seemed to be yearning for something—but what? All she knew was that she was close to begging if she didn't receive it soon.

Leisurely he began nibbling her all over like she was some rare delicacy to be savored and enjoyed. Surprisingly, she found she was offering herself to him without any feelings of embarrassment or shame—just the innocence of pure love to be given freely and unselfishly. When he reached the juncture where her thighs touched together, he lightly brushed soft kisses across the soft, curly black hair of her apex.

Now he was so close she could reach up and entwine her fingers in the dark auburn locks of hair curling softly around his shoulders while his fingers gently searched, then probed the very center of her being. This caused her to be filled with an urgent need and she arched, seeking his hand, thus allowing him better access. She was wiggling and moaning and about to call out his name—

Suddenly, she awoke and found she was in a heated sweat, with her breathing labored and her heart racing like a wild stallion across the Scottish moors. Now she felt more disturbed than before. She asked herself, *Who is the man who seems to know me most intimately and leaves me breathlessly yearning for more? Is he someone I really know, or is it just someone I dreamed up in my imagination?*

12

Summer 1705

Near Inverness, Scotland

AS THEY RODE WITHIN A couple miles of Inverness, Colwyn thought to himself, *Thank God we are almost there!* He knew his men were grateful of the fact as he had ridden them hard the past few days and they all needed rest. Also the horses desperately needed to be refreshed after being on the trail so long. In his eagerness to get there as soon as possible, Colwyn had only allowed them to stop for a few hours at a time since starting on this journey.

Finally the town was in sight and eagerly Colwyn headed straight for the Inverness Inn. He flicked a coin to a young boy standing outside and asked him to see to having the horses taken care of at the stables. A broad grin flashed across his dirty little face as he hurried to his task.

Dismounting, Colwyn headed straight inside, in search of the innkeeper.

"Good day to you, sir," the owner greeted him. "How may I help you today?"

"My name is Colwyn Campbell and I need four rooms for myself and my seven men. Do you have that many available?"

"Yes, sir, as a matter of fact I do," the innkeeper responded with a smile. "Do you have any baggage that needs to be taken up?"

"No," Colwyn answered curtly. "We'll only be here for a short time. If it is not too much trouble, could we please have some heated water for baths and shaves?"

"Right away, sir. If you'll just sign in, I'll get your room keys. So you're just passing through then?" the innkeeper continued curiously. "Where are you headed?"

"Actually," Colwyn answered, "I'm looking for someone; a man by the name of Ian Douglas. Do you know how I can find him?"

The innkeeper immediately became suspicious and fairly shouted at Colwyn, "Ian Douglas! "What do you want with him?"

"I've heard of his extraordinary abilities and I've come to ask him for his help," Colwyn announced.

"From whom and where did you here of Ian?" the innkeeper asked.

"A man by the name of Alexander Buchanan told me of his talents and the story of the lost boy. He is a close friend of mine and he told me to seek you out for information on Ian's whereabouts," Colwyn explained.

The innkeeper didn't know whether to believe Colwyn or not but he did remember the man by the name of Alexander Buchanan. He had been a recent customer of his. However, he didn't know if this man's intentions were honorable even though he certainly looked like a man of quality. *The question is,* he asked himself, *could this man be the type that would hurt my friend? There have been many witch-hunters who have looked for him in the past. Yet, this one certainly doesn't fit their description though. Could it be a trick?*

Deciding to go with his instincts, the innkeeper replied ominously, "I must warn you that Ian don't like nobody coming 'round trying to bother him. Even if you did happen to find him, he'd probably shoot you before you came within 100 feet of his door."

"I really need to find him," Colwyn determinedly uttered as he grabbed the innkeeper's collar and pulled him within an inch of his face. "I'm a man desperate for his help! If you won't help me I'll search until I find someone who will. I haven't come this far to just give up now!"

The innkeeper could clearly see the determination hidden behind the silent, almost desperate, plea in Colwyn's eyes, and decided to help him. Besides, he didn't relish the fact the man looked as if he would strangle him to death at any moment.

"Now, hold on a minute!" the innkeeper exclaimed as he tried to release himself from Colwyn's tight hold. "I didn't say I *wouldn't* help you. I just wanted to let you know you'd be met with resistance. Ian prefers to be left to himself. A peculiar one is he."

"Despite his wanting to be left alone, I really must speak with him," Colwyn confessed. "This is a most urgent matter. Actually, it concerns the most important person in my life." (He found he had already begun to think of Lysette in that way.) "Can you understand that?" Colwyn added to his final plea.

"I think I can understand when a person is desperate enough to try anything and that's why I'm going to tell you where to find Ian Douglas. He lives in a small hut in the woods about ten miles from here. I'll draw you a map with the directions. Though you shouldn't have too much trouble finding him, again I'm going to warn you to be on your guard. Ian don't like *nobody* poking around his place."

"I appreciate your help very much," Colwyn told him. "You could never guess how much this means to me."

"I think I can," the innkeeper replied. "I just hope you find what you're looking for. Not many people have much luck with Ian."

Quickly the innkeeper changed the subject saying, "Your rooms are on the second floor, Mr. Campbell. They're the last four at the end of the hallway. I'll have the maids heat up some water right away and bring it up to your rooms. Would you want to be having something to eat before you head out, sir?"

"Yes, that would be fine," Colwyn answered.

"Would you prefer to come down and eat or would you prefer to have it sent up to your rooms?"

"We would like it sent up, thank you," Colwyn smiled his gratefulness.

Eagerly he turned and then bounded up the steps to his room. All the while he thought, *The faster I am refreshed, the faster I can get back to the business of finding Lysette.*

* * *

It was soon obvious to Colwyn that what the innkeeper had told him was true. They had headed out right after eating and had no trouble following the directions on the map. As soon as they reached a clearing though, they had to tie up the horses and leave them behind because the trail was too overgrown to maneuver them through the area safely. In fact, they had to cut back prickly bushes and brambles just to push themselves through.

The whole time Colwyn had been keeping a sharp eye out, or so he thought, as Ian's traps were cleverly disguised and hidden. One of his men in the rear having tripped a wire had been yanked up in a net. It had taken them precious minutes they could ill afford to spare, freeing him. Then another one of his men took a wrong turn and fell into a dugout hole that had been cleverly covered over with tree limbs. It took more of their time to pull him back up.

It is a good thing there are eight of us, Colwyn thought, *otherwise, Mr. Douglas could have easily put an effective end to anyone reaching him. I have to admit he is an expert in keeping everyone at bay.*

Finally, they spotted a dilapidated, obscure little hut, hoping it was the old hermit's. A few minutes later, without any more mishaps, Colwyn let out a sigh of relief. Though he hurried his steps in order to reach the hut, he wasn't about to let down his guard. Upon arriving he noted the place looked neglected and deserted; but Colwyn knew looks could be deceiving. Besides, he had a feeling the old man was in there watching every move they made. He didn't think anybody could really be able to slip up on Ian Douglas without him being aware of it.

While Colwyn knocked on the unwelcoming door, he wondered just what to expect next. Naturally, there was no answer. Though he was met with only silence, he was determined not to let it deter him.

"Mr. Douglas, my name is Colwyn Campbell!" he shouted through the cracks. "I haven't come here to cause you any harm. I've only come here to ask for your help."

Still silence reigned.

"Mr. Douglas, I won't go away. If I have to, I'll camp out here by your door for as long as it takes . . . until I can get a response from you."

Finally a response came from within. "You might as well go away for I can do nothing to help you!" the old man called out gruffly. "So just go on back to wherever you came from."

"I'm afraid I can't do that, Mr. Douglas. I've come all the way from Edinburgh and I haven't come this far just to be similarly dismissed." Colwyn continued speaking in spite of his resistant audience. "A friend told me of your abilities. He said you helped find a lost little boy."

"So, what has that got to do with you?" the old man bellowed. "I distinctly remember telling you to leave. If you're not gone from here in the next few moments, I promise you will regret it!"

Ian was really becoming unfriendly and irritable, from the tone of his voice.

"I can't leave, sir." Colwyn decided to resort to a little desperate pleading as nothing was reaching this man so far. "I've come in regards of my fiancée, a woman I happen to love very much and will try anything to get her back. She is missing, Mr. Douglas, but it isn't from natural causes. Someone sent her away—" Colwyn paused there but again the old man remained mute. "It was a witch, sir," Colwyn continued again. "A conniving little witch cast a spell and she vanished into thin air."

There seemed to be quite a ruckus inside before the door was suddenly jerked open. Colwyn thought for a moment he must be hallucinating as the man who stood before him resembled something of a specter. His hair was long and white, his clothes were filthy and they looked as if he slept in them. The beard he sported was just as white and hung down to the top of his knees.

"Don't just stand there like a bunch of dull-witted buffoons!" the specter spoke. "Get yourselves on in here. I don't intend to stand in the doorway all night. The air is chilly out there."

Colwyn didn't wait for a second command. He was in the door before the old man could change his mind. The rest of his troop followed suit.

"You'll have to pardon my earlier rudeness. You see, I don't normally take to strangers." This was Ian's way of offering an excuse.

Gesturing to some rickety chairs placed around an old table, Ian said, "Well, go ahead and have a seat. You all make me a mite nervous standing around lurking in the shadows."

They all sat down slowly and carefully, not quite trusting the sturdiness of their seats.

"A witch you say?" Ian addressed Colwyn. "You'll have to tell me everything you know about the spell she used if I'm to help you."

"I'm afraid I can't tell you much. I didn't witness the act."

Colwyn hadn't taken his eyes off Ian since first setting foot in the hut. He seemed to know quite a bit about witchcraft and Colwyn was still reeling from the fact that all it took was the mention of that subject for him to do a complete turnabout and open up his door to them.

"My stable-boy saw the whole thing and he told me of it," Colwyn continued his explanation.

"Is your stable-boy with you?" Ian asked.

"Unfortunately, no. He's back at home in Edinburgh tending to his duties. My father had a greater need for him there. My fiancée's father has fallen ill and he has provided an invaluable service during this crisis by running errands."

Ian became thoughtful for a moment then asked, "Do you think he remembered the words that she used?"

"I don't really know," Colwyn confessed. "All he told me was that they were words he didn't understand."

"Probably that's surely because they were ancient," Ian reflected. Then he told Colwyn, "I'll have to speak to him myself. Maybe he'll remember something. Even if he thinks it's insignificant, it could be very pertinent. I'll definitely need more information; otherwise, I won't be able to do you much good. So, I guess we'd better get ready to ride. I'm going back to Edinburgh with you."

Ian made this last statement rather matter-of-factly.

At Ian's words, Colwyn felt as if a great weight had just fallen from his shoulders. The feeling even over-powered the shock of Ian's last statement.

"Thank you," he uttered simply and sincerely.

Finally, he was beginning to believe a miracle could be accomplished and Lysette was nearer to being found.

Ian told him, "Now, I have something more to ask you. Do you have an object that belongs to her on which I can concentrate?"

Colwyn thought for a moment; then he remembered. "Yes, I have a piece of her jewelry. It's an amethyst bracelet and it's one of her favorites." As he spoke, Colwyn pulled it from the pouch he had been carrying in the inside pocket of his jacket then willingly handed it over into Ian's outstretched hand.

"Good," Ian said grasping it tightly. "Has she worn this recently?"

"Yes," Colwyn answered. "She wore it a few days before she disappeared. We were on a picnic and the clasp broke. I took it from her, promising to have it fixed. I had forgotten about it until now. All my energies have been focused on getting her back."

Suddenly a picture flashed into his mind of how lovely she looked that day and a smile crossed his features for the first time in days.

"I've found the more recent they've had contact with an object, the easier and stronger the vision comes to me," Ian interrupted Colwyn's beautiful memory with his explanation.

"I'll need to be alone now. It's better if I'm in the dark and there is complete silence. That way no distractions can interfere with the process."

"Would you like us to wait outside?" Colwyn politely asked.

"No, no, that's all right. I have a dark room in the back I use when I meditate. I should only be gone a short while. Then I'll come back and tell you what I can . . . if anything," he added dauntingly as he stalked off.

Colwyn waited on the edge of his chair for Ian's return; all the while hoping the man would have success.

Ian proved to be true to his word as he returned only a few short minutes later. To Colwyn though, it had seemed like an eternity. He hadn't realized he'd been holding his breath waiting anxiously for Ian to speak until he felt it expel slowly at Ian's first words.

"Well, I can say this," Ian finally uttered after staring into the young man's eyes a few tense seconds. "She has a very strong presence, this fiancée of yours, and quite beautiful I might add."

So far, thought Colwyn, *he isn't saying anything I didn't already know.*

"But I'm afraid," Ian continued rather ominously, "the news I have to impart, you might not find very promising."

Colwyn jumped up in alarm as if his whole world had come crashing down with the imparting of Ian's ominous words, "Don't go getting all crazy on me now!"

Ian tried to calm Colwyn and said, "Before you ask, she's still alive and in Edinburgh."

Colwyn was now puzzled; he didn't think that that was bad news at all.

"The problem is," Ian added, "she's three hundred years into the future."

13

Summer 2005

Edinburgh, Scotland

HAVING SPENT A VERY RESTLESS night, Lysette got up early the next morning only to find the three roommates already up. They were busily running around the apartment like a passel of chickens with their heads chopped off. Observing all the rapid activity, Lysette thought to herself, *If having a job means acting as if the world would come to an end if you didn't get there on time, then I'm glad I don't have one.*

Lorna was busy making breakfast for them all while Stacy and Susan kept the bathroom monopolized. Lysette decided she would see if she could help Lorna.

When she walked through to the kitchen, Lorna greeted her cheerily, "Good morning, Lisa. Did you sleep well?"

"I'm afraid not as well as I hoped," Lysette confessed after realizing the unfamiliar name was indeed directed at her. She hoped she would get used to it if her memory didn't soon return. "I kept tossing and turning but it wasn't because I found your bed to be uncomfortable," she rushed to explain when she saw the distress on Lorna's face. "Actually, I found it very comfortable indeed. It was just that a reoccurring dream kept waking me up . . . it was rather disturbing."

"What was the dream about? Did you recognize anything?" Lorna asked her as she continued fixing the morning meal.

"No . . . and I couldn't make any sense of it either," Lysette answered.

"Do you want to talk about it?" Lorna asked her with both concern and curiosity.

Taking a deep sigh, Lysette replied, "Not right now. I'm not sure it means anything."

Actually, Lysette knew she wouldn't be comfortable discussing the hauntingly handsome man that was disturbing her dreams.

"I'm so sorry you spent a rough night," Lorna apologized as she smiled sympathetically at Lysette. She didn't want to push her or make her feel uncomfortable. "Maybe it was because this is an unfamiliar place. I promise you'll sleep like a log tonight. But for now I've got just the cure for you; a good hot breakfast," she offered.

"I really don't feel all that hungry but is there something I can do to help you right now?" Lysette told her.

"No, darling, I've got everything covered for now and don't give me any more nonsense about not feeling hungry. You need to eat in order to keep up your strength."

Leading Lysette to a chair at the table, Lorna indicated she should sit. When Lysette complied, Lorna placed a hot plate of eggs, bacon, and toast in front of her. Then she handed her a glass of orange juice and a cup of coffee. The appetizing aroma of the food and coffee finally got to Lysette as it wafted up her nostrils. She waited no longer and began digging into the heaped plate of food.

"Stacy and Susan will be through in the bathroom soon," Lorna explained. "Then you can have your turn.

That's the only inconvenience of this place—having only one *small* bathroom with three women living here."

Lysette was only beginning to understand just what she meant. She was still reeling from the fact that heated water actually flowed from the pipes straight into the tub with just a turn of a faucet. She would be glad when her turn finally arrived.

"So you won't feel too uneasy or uncomfortable, I'm going to be staying here with you today," Lorna explained. "Stacy and Susan are going to cover for me at the office. They don't mind a little extra work and as long as the work gets done, the bosses don't mind." She snickered slightly as she said this.

"This morning we're going to go out in the neighborhood and post your picture to see if we can draw out anybody who recognizes you. If so, they can contact the police station. We're also going to stop by there just in case they've found out something by now and haven't contacted us yet. Dr. Warner may also call today with the results of your test so I'll leave the answering machine on while we're out," Lorna finally finished explaining.

Lysette just nodded her head in agreement since most of what Lorna was talking about just flew right over her head anyway.

* * *

Lorna and Lysette didn't have any luck with the posters. They were out and about on the streets and were disappointed when nobody recognized Lysette. Even so, they went ahead and tacked up the flyers, hoping sometime in the near future they would get a response.

They stopped by the police station but there wasn't any news there either and Lysette was beginning to feel the day would have been fairly grim if it hadn't been for all the wondrous sights she observed around the city. There was the ever-present sound of the cars driving by on the busy streets, the horns the drivers blew when they seemed to be angry at other drivers, were noises she felt she should be familiar with but wasn't. She was sure it was something new to her and somehow knew it to be so. Everywhere she looked people were rushing about on sidewalks and in crossways with little oblong objects pressed to their ears shouting to be overheard.

When Lorna observed Lysette's interest in them. She explained: "They are cell phones and the modern-day world could not live without them."

At this statement Lysette gave her a skeptical look and Lorna snickered at her expression. She went on to further explain: "I don't mean it literally; it is just that the people who own them have become so dependent on the freedom it gives them; not having to hunt or go find a land line."

Glancing at Lysette, Lorna saw she looked as if she were about to develop a headache from all the information. Lorna then told her, "I will better explain it later on tonight."

Lysette did ask her though, "Why don't you think it necessary to carry around a cell phone like everyone else?"

Confessing her weakness, Lorna explained, "I just can't seem to stay within my minutes and not go over. Even with the 1500 plan, I talk too much and I can't afford the overage charges any more. Stacy and Susan made me cancel my service and do without for a while. I swear they are worse than Army drill sergeants!"

Lysette smiled and though she felt a little sorry for

her new-found friend, she felt certain Stacy and Susan were only looking out for Lorna's well being.

*   *   *

Thankfully, Lysette felt cool and comfortable in her borrowed cotton blouse and woven polyester slacks on that hot summer day. She thought to herself, *And to think I almost hadn't worn them since I wasn't used to women wearing what I considered to be a man's attire. But the prospect had been a little too intriguing and appealing for me to pass up. Now I'm glad I didn't.*

The day turned out not to be a total loss, however. As the two young ladies arrived home later that afternoon, Dr. Warner called with the results of her CAT Scan. There had been no signs of a tumor or any other head trauma. He therefore diagnosed Lysette's memory loss as possibly psychological or shock induced and said he would like to schedule a psychotherapy session for her the next Tuesday at 3:00 P.M.

After briefly explaining things to Lysette, Lorna informed her she would take off work early that Tuesday and take her to the appointment.

Though Lysette heard what Lorna told her, she was at a total loss as to what a "psychotherapy session" was and how it could help her. Patiently, Lorna explained it the best she could, but Lysette still was not convinced that just talking to that man under what Lorna said was "a state of hypnosis," would unlock the secrets of her mind. However, she decided that if it made Lorna happy, she would try it.

Also, she kept thinking about the man in her dreams and wondering who he was. She was a little frightened yet couldn't help wonder: *If this "hypnosis" gets me to mention him, then what might it mean? What would they think if I described the dream to them? Would they be able to determine if he is real or a figment of my imagination?*

To be honest with herself, right then Lysette wasn't confident she wanted to find out. Whenever she thought of him it was with a sense of mixed feelings and emotions. Not only was there an immediate feeling of excitement, but there also seemed to be a nagging sense of fear; as if knowing him might somehow put her life, or his, in jeopardy. Since she didn't understand any of it she didn't want to delve too deeply into it at this point. Vaguely there seemed to be something in her heart telling her he meant a great deal to her and she yearned for his existence in her life.

There had been times when she looked around at the faces in the crowd, hoping she would recognize him. In her mind she kept imagining him riding up on a magnificent black steed, reaching down, lifting her up and tucking her firmly in front of him on the horse. It would have been such a valiant rescue and one she realized she would have readily accepted. Several times she had shaken her head to try and clear her thoughts and return to "real life." Something told her she might be treading on dangerous ground to be dreaming so often.

* * *

Stacy and Susan arrived home a little while later and since neither one had felt like cooking that night, they had brought Chinese take-out for supper. Lysette thoroughly enjoyed her meal but soon began feeling tired. She was still a little worn out from her restless night before, and her very active day. Before she could get a taste of her fortune cookie, she was unabashedly stretching and yawning.

Lorna suggested: “Lisa, I want you stay in my room during the duration of your stay with us. I think you will sleep better.” Lysette was too tired to argue.

The three friends bid her good night, but then Lorna surprised Lysette by asking her, “Will you be all right if we leave you alone in the apartment tomorrow? I hate to miss another day at work and put the extra workload on Stacy and Susan.”

The three friends insisted they didn’t mind if Lysette felt too uncomfortable to be left alone but Lysette assured them: “Go ahead. I will be fine by myself.”

After saying good night, Lysette headed down the hallway to Lorna’s room. She wondered, *Why am I acting so brave when I’ve never been more scared in my life?*

14

Summer 1705

Outside Inverness, Scotland

COLWYN WAS POSITIVELY FLOORED BY Ian's last statement and his voice was raised and very forceful when he blurted out in disbelief, "That's impossible! How could you possibly say that? People just don't travel through time!"

This could not be happening. I have to be dreaming, Colwyn told himself almost convincingly.

Ian ended the younger man's wishful thinking by insisting, "I'm afraid it *is* possible and very real. Don't ever underestimate the power of witchcraft. It is an evil force that is very potent and it will take all our strength and know-how to combat it," Ian remarked warningly.

He continued, "In my vision I saw her quite clearly. If your fiancée has long, dark, luscious hair and an extraordinary pair of purple eyes, then that's her. She was relaxing in a room. Not seeing anyone else, I assumed she was alone. The room is very unusual looking," Ian went on to explain while Colwyn listened intently to his every word. "I've never seen the likes of any place like it in my life. It was filled with objects of which I have no explanation but she seemed quite comfortable and unharmed," he added reassuringly.

Colwyn let go a sigh of relief at this information and in joy exclaimed, "Thank God, she's all right!"

"I saw a paper with printed words on it resting on a table in front of her," Ian informed with further details. "It had the date August 2, 2005 on it. I haven't been keeping up with the days but I know the year we're in is 1705. Now to me, that's three hundred years ahead of our time."

Colwyn didn't know what to make of all this. *Every time I think I'm closer, she seems to get further and further away. How am I ever to overcome this insurmountable obstacle? Could things get much worse?* he thought to himself.

Out loud he asked Ian, "Is there anything that can be done to reverse the spell?" Even to him, Colwyn's voice was beginning to sound desperate.

"I believe I'll be able to help you," Ian answered, "but we'll have to act fast if we're to accomplish the impossible. As I see it, the longer she is in that time period, the more she will become a part of it. After a certain amount of time has passed it will no longer be possible to bring her home. She would become trapped in that time forever."

"What do we have to do to prevent this?" Colwyn shouted anxiously.

"We must get ready to leave right away," Ian told him. "But first I must learn everything I can about the spell that was used."

Colwyn didn't hesitate for even a half second. He gave the order to depart for Edinburgh.

* * *

The nine riders made good time after they got under way that day. Even Ian, in his advanced age, was able to keep up with the best of them. Observing him, Colwyn thought, *There isn't one slow thing about him.*

Because of the urgent need for haste, Colwyn hadn't been able to speak with Ian any further. But that was a situation he intended to correct as soon as they stopped to rest for the night. He had a thousand and one questions with no answers.

Finally night began to fall and it would soon be too dark to see and ride safely. Colwyn found a copse amongst some trees where he felt they would be safe. Some of the men eagerly set up camp while the others went hunting for their dinner in the forest. After they had dined on wild boar, Mac and the rest of his men prepared for a few hours of rest. They bid Colwyn and Ian a good night and since they all were very tired, fell asleep almost immediately when they stretched out on their makeshift pallets.

On the other hand, since the day of Lysette's disappearance, Colwyn had been unable to sleep very soundly so was still wide-awake. Ian, living alone, was used to not having to answer to anyone and spent most nights staying up to all hours working on whatever he had a mind to. Thus he also was awake and not ready for sleep.

Colwyn was glad he finally had a chance to converse with Ian alone and without any interruptions. This gave him a chance to discuss the matters uppermost in his mind. They were sitting by the fireside, watching the embers of the now fading flames, when Colwyn took the opportunity to speak up.

He began by saying, "I'm sure you've guessed I have a good many questions floating around in my head but am not sure what to ask first."

Ian chuckled a little at Colwyn's first statement to him that night and responded, "Yes, I can surely imagine and I'll try to answer them the best I can. For now, I'll give you what information I have. From what you've told me so far, and in my vision where I saw her in a future time, I'm taking an educated guess that some sort of time-transference spell was used on her. I won't be able to know much more until I learn what spell the woman used. I don't suppose there is any way you can get the witch who did this to tell us now, is there?" Ian had been very serious when he had asked Colwyn this question as he hoped there would be an avenue to pursue there.

Picking up a little on Ian's train of thought, Colwyn answered, "I doubt it. The last time I saw Felicia she wasn't exactly in a very helpful mood."

He then gave Ian the details of his last meeting with Felicia.

"Well, I can believe that," Ian uttered after Colwyn finished with his tale. "She sounds like a very disturbed young woman. Is there anyone who might be able to reason with her?"

"Her father might be able to get her to talk," Colwyn uttered this thought to Ian. "He's the one that told me of your extraordinary abilities. I believe he was trying to make up for his daughter's evil deed."

"How did he know of my existence?" Ian then asked Colwyn. "I don't recall knowing anyone from Edinburgh."

Colwyn told him, "He was up in Inverness when you helped find that little boy. His name is Alexander Buchanan."

"I've never met him but he has my sympathies," Ian responded. "Now, can you tell me the reason why this witch sent Lysette off?"

"I suppose she thought she could win my love and have me all to herself; but I've never made her such a promise," Colwyn explained. "I've had a former relationship with her and for the life of me I can't understand why

I did. When we were younger, I always thought of her as a little sister. As we grew older, she became clinging and needy to the point where I was annoyed with her most of the time. Anyway, she got the notion into her head that I rejected her when Lysette arrived and she became insanely jealous. She must have devised the plot soon after Lysette came to the castle."

"Sometimes, it doesn't take much for a woman to believe she's been spurned for another," Ian reflected. "You know the old saying: Hell hath no fury like a woman scorned."

"Yes, I've found that out firsthand," Colwyn responded.

After gazing into the fire for a few moments in deep thought, Colwyn then said, "I think I should warn you there's another obstacle to combat in this problem. Felicia informed me, right before I left her and headed for you and Inverness, that she had given Lysette a potion that would cause her to suffer memory loss. Is there anything you can give her to restore it when we get her back?" (Colwyn was absolutely convinced they would recover her.)

"That is definitely not good," Ian retorted at hearing this last bit of news. "It has been my experience that nothing brings back memories besides time itself. The brain has a way of healing itself but it is not an overnight miracle. It will take time for it to reassemble what it has lost. But I must tell you now, that it is most imperative that she remember you *before* we can bring her back."

"Why is that?" Colwyn asked, now becoming somewhat alarmed at Ian's insistence on this point.

"Can't we just deal with the situation once she's back here with us?" Colwyn asked.

"I'm afraid we won't be able to do that, now. With her memory gone, I wouldn't be able to bring her back."

Colwyn was about to burst out an expletive at Ian's words but Ian noticed his expression and forestalled him by saying, "I would be unable to bring her back . . ." He continued after a moment saying, "But I believe I might be able to send *you* forward to that time and you could retrieve her."

Leaning closer, Colwyn remained silent and listened attentively as Ian explained. "You see, Lysette has no idea she doesn't belong in that time period. Therefore, *she* has to *want* to come home before I can bring her. That's why I must send you; so you can convince her. There has to be something she remembers in order for her to desire to return and that something has to be you. She has to *believe* in the power or it will all be for naught. If that doesn't happen, she will live out the rest of her days in that time frame if it cannot be done. The bottom line is this: Her love for you must be stronger than the evil that sent her there."

After those ominous words, Colwyn prayed to God that her love was strong enough for him.

Before he and Ian made ready to turn in for the night, Colwyn had to ask one last question; one that had been on his mind ever since Ian had a change of heart and jerked the door open suddenly in front of them. "Ian, what was it I said that made you decide to help me?"

"For me to answer that completely, you'll have to know a little bit about me," Ian stated.

After a few moments gazing into the flames, he began: "Close to five years ago I was engaged to a very loving, giving, gentle, beautiful lady. I'd been a bachelor for most of my life, and then she walked in. At the time I owned and operated a small bookstore. I was also the local apothecary. One day I looked up and there she stood, a vision come to life. One look in her eyes and I was lost. She was a widow who had moved to town in order to begin a new life and become the schoolteacher. And low and behold, to my utter amazement, she was also smitten with me as well. It was a sweet and lovely courtship and my head floated in the clouds every second I was with her.

"One day we were spending a quiet afternoon strolling hand in hand down the country lane, just enjoying being in love when suddenly some storm clouds started rolling in and decided to drop a downpour on us. We got caught in the sudden torrents of heavy rainwater and ran under a cluster of trees in order to try and escape being totally soaked. Never unclasping our hands the whole time, we were barely under the tree a second before it struck. That one streak of lightening lit up the whole sky. I didn't know what was happening as it surged through my body . . . just remember feeling numb afterwards. It must have knocked me out for a short while as I recall waking up even though it was a few moments before I could move.

"By then it had stopped raining and when I was able to get my limbs to move, I rolled over to my Annabelle—that was her name, Annabelle, and not a better name could have suited her more. I figured she must have been knocked out also as she was so still just lying there. I shook her, trying to get her to wake but I could not get any reaction from her. Picking her up I carried her in my arms all the way back to town. The doctor there tried his best, but later told me there had been nothing he could do for her, as she was gone. Evidently the lightning went right through my body, straight into hers through our linked hands before it exited out her feet. Whereas the strike had only rendered me unconscious, it had killed her immediately."

Ian paused on this sad note and took a deep breath. Colwyn felt a deep sympathy for his loss but was loath to interrupt. The older man read it all over his face though and then continued. "Soon after the accident, I discovered I had acquired this strange power. It started out with my being able to see in my mind, where things were located after I had lost them. I thought my memory was improving until I discovered I could see where other people's lost articles were after they mentioned the problem to me.

"At first, they were very grateful when I told them where they could find their lost items. A little later, though, they became frightened and somewhat suspicious of me because I was rarely ever wrong. It seemed to them I knew a little too much about things I shouldn't and they began to accuse me of practicing witchcraft and finally drove me out of the town.

"I must admit, I became rather bitter and angry after that. First, losing Annabelle that way, and then the whole town turning against me. I locked up the store, built me a little hut up in the woods and left civilization behind me. As long as I kept to myself and didn't show my face in town very much, the town folk left me alone. I still have a few loyal friends who still believe in me and help out. This has to be done in secret, as I don't want them to be ostracized like me. Old Eddie, the innkeeper, is one of them."

"Yes, I figured that out when I spoke to him," Colwyn told him. "He came across as very protective of your privacy until I was able to convince him to tell us where to find you."

"You must be all right then if Old Eddie was impressed enough to tell you," Ian said with gleeful banter.

He then turned serious and after gazing again into the fire resumed his tale. "I had a lot of time to think while alone in the hut. After a time, I figured that if I was going to be accused of witchcraft I might as well learn as much as I could about how to master something over which I had no control . . . yet. In my store I had had a few books about ancient spells and potions so read every one of them and began to practice a few incantations . . . nothing that would bring harm to anyone. Actually, I only tried them on myself. My knowledge as an apothecary came in handy when mixing potions for my experiments.

"I hadn't had much contact with anyone in the town until the day when the young couple who lost their little boy showed up on my doorstep. It was pure desperation that had led them to me only after exhausting every other means they thought possible. Obviously they loved their son more than they were frightened of me. After I found him, the townspeople began to soften and change their attitude slightly towards me. As for me, I'm afraid I've been rather unforgiving of their former treatment.

"That is until you showed up at my door with your story. It hit me smack dab in a place I had long thought was dead. The loneliness in your voice moved me and I just couldn't ignore it. Though I tried, I lost. The sound of love coming from your heart reached my heart and all I could see was Annabelle and the last smile she had given me. Then I knew what I must do. What Annabelle wanted me to do was open that door and help you."

"But you helped that couple when they asked," Colwyn pointed out.

"I had my own selfish reason for doing that," Ian confessed. "I wanted to prove to the townspeople how wrong they had been about me. But with you, it's different. I want to help you get your fiancée back. Annabelle would have liked that because now I feel my heart is beginning to reawaken. Somehow I feel her presence close to me and I haven't felt this alive in years.

“I suggest we get some shut eye now,” Ian gruffly said changing the subject quickly, slapping his hand across his knee as he rose. “We want to be up with the sun, to get a bright and early start.”

As Colwyn watched Ian, he thought the older man seemed a little embarrassed at his emotional confession and was a little uncomfortable with someone witnessing the tears now forming at the corners of his eyes.

Respecting the man’s privacy and emotions, Colwyn made no comment but agreed one hundred percent with getting some sleep and rising early on the morn.

15

CASTLE CAMPBELL WAS A WELCOME sight to Colwyn when the group of men finally arrived late in the afternoon. He knew Jeremy would be in the stables conducting his usual duties at this time of day. Colwyn was anxious to speak with him first thing in the hopes he would be able to shed additional light on Lysette's disappearance.

As soon as Colwyn entered the stable, Jeremy spotted him. He put aside his pitchfork with a welcoming smile as he hurried over to his employer saying, "Milord, it's good to see you return home. Everybody has missed you. Would you like me to attend to Satan personally, sir?"

"In a moment, Jeremy. Right now, I'd like to speak with you a bit," Colwyn said looking down at the boy with a friendly expression.

"Think back to the day when you witnessed the Mistress Felicia uttering the incantation to Mistress Lysette in the gardens. Do you happen to remember *any* of the words Felicia spoke when she made the Mistress Lysette disappear?"

"Golly, Milord, I'm really sorry. I was so scared at what I saw that I was concentrating mostly on them not catching me there. Not a single word of the gibberish that witch was spouting out could I understand." Jeremy was genuinely apologetic and appeared a little upset at his inability to help further.

"That's all right, Jeremy, I appreciate all you've told me of what you know. It has helped tremendously and don't you worry about a thing. We'll just find another way," Colwyn said to Jeremy as he ruffled the top of his head with his hand in an effort to comfort him.

Though Colwyn was disappointed at this news, he didn't want the boy to realize this and add to his discomfort.

Turning to Ian who was sitting on his horse right beside him Colwyn said, "It looks as if we have no other choice now. We'll just have to find some way to get Felicia to confess."

"Let's freshen up and have a decent meal first," Ian responded as he dismounted his steed and let Jeremy take the reigns to give the horse some much needed attention and refreshment. "I know you will never admit it but you look beat and exhausted. You need to rest and I don't want you to argue with me about it," Ian went on to say before Colwyn could make his protest. "You will need all your strength to face what has to be done next. Your Lysette has only you to count on and you won't be doing her any good if you collapse at her feet."

Colwyn couldn't protest that point so just nodded his head slightly in agreement.

"Then we can ride over to where Felicia lives. If we're lucky, maybe she'll have a change of heart and tell you what you yearn to know," Ian finished.

To himself Colwyn thought, *The probability of that is definitely doubtful but one can always hope for a miracle.* Out loud he said, "That's a good idea, Ian. I need to speak to my father now anyhow. I'm sure he's extremely anxious to hear any news. Also, I'd like to introduce you to him. I have a feeling you two will take an instant liking to one another. You remind me of him in so many ways."

"Is that so?" Ian replied, a little flattered. "I am extremely honored by your comparison and I'd be happy to meet your father."

"Well, let's be on our way then," Colwyn said slapping Ian on the back in a friendly gesture. "Now that you've mentioned it, I realize I'm starved."

Ian nodded his approval and they walked through the open stable doors with purposeful strides. Colwyn found he was a little hard pressed to keep up with Ian and briefly wondered to himself, *How can a man of his obvious age came up with so much energy . . . especially after being on the back of a horse all day?*

Colwyn found his father in his study, this time of day as usual, while strolling in without even bothering to knock. Angus Campbell had never been so glad to see anyone in his life, as he was when he clapped eyes on his son minutes after his return.

"Father, I'm back," the son announced broadly, "and I have someone with me I'd like for you to meet."

Normally Angus was not a demonstrative man but he was so overcome with emotion at this first sight of his son in over a week that he jumped up quickly, ran around his desk and clasped his son firmly in a tight bear hug with his well-built muscled arm "Colwyn, I'm so glad you've returned safe and sound. I've been rather worried with no word from you."

Colwyn was a little surprised at his father's show of affection but couldn't help feeling pleased that his father loved him enough to worry.

Realizing he was holding his son a little too tightly, Angus tried to brush off his embarrassment as he stepped back and coughed a little as he said in what he considered his most authoritative tone, "Well, Colwyn, what news have you to impart? I hope it is good for I have had enough bad news to last me a lifetime."

Understanding his father perfectly well, Colwyn then proceeded to introduce Ian and explained the circumstances and importance of having to deal with Felicia again. Since Angus had found out from Colwyn's messenger all about Ian's abilities, he silently prayed he would be able to help them. Colwyn had been correct about the two men liking one another right away. It did not take long for them to find out they had quite a bit in common as they spoke a little later.

Angus informed Colwyn and Ian that Asa was still not in good health and the doctor had told him he probably wouldn't begin to recover until his daughter was back home safe and sound. After this bit of news, Colwyn was even more anxious to head out to Buchanan Castle.

Before leaving, they were offered a meal, which the hungry men didn't refuse. While they partook of the delicious fare, Angus sat with them and used this time to get to know Ian better. He found he trusted this odd man with an age-old instinct he couldn't explain properly in words. It was just something he felt inside.

* * *

Colwyn sensed something was not quite right even before they came within sight of the Buchanan Castle gates. It was nothing he could see, just a feeling so strong it nearly overwhelmed him. As they approached, everything seemed much too quiet and Colwyn felt as if the tiny hairs on the back of his neck were standing on end while his nerves tingled as they sent out a warning. There was a somber quality in the air around the castle and Colwyn understood why a little while later as they walked up to the front door and spotted the enormous wreath hanging upon it. The family was in mourning.

Dear God, thought Colwyn, *could Felicia have murdered her own father? Could I really put it past her after what she has already done?* Suddenly Colwyn found he was praying it wasn't true. *Alexander is the only one who could have persuaded Felicia to give me the needed information. Without her father my mission is useless because I know she will never willingly help me now.*

It seemed as if an eternity passed as he stood waiting for an answer to his summons. He couldn't understand the delay as he had practically banged the big brass knocker off the door.

Finally a manservant arrived and opened the door, too slowly for Colwyn's liking. "How do you do, gentlemen?" the manservant directly addressed Colwyn and Ian. "How may I help you?"

"We are very sorry to intrude in this time of sorrow. I am Colwyn Campbell, neighbor of Lord Buchanan, and this is my friend, Mr. Ian Douglas," Colwyn informed the manservant as he didn't recognize him as one of the Buchanan's regular employees. He figured the man must not have had the position very long, which came as no surprise, since Felicia usually managed to drive off most of the good help with her mean, spoiled, and discourteous attitude. "We would like to speak with Lord Buchanan on a most urgent matter, if it is at all possible. Is he in?"

"He is in, sir, but I'm afraid he's not receiving any visitors at this time," the manservant retorted in a brusque standoffish manner.

Colwyn found himself momentarily relieved at discovering the old gentleman was still alive.

"He is in deep mourning over his loss and wishes not to be disturbed," the manservant continued.

"Good God! His loss, that could only mean . . ." Colwyn didn't like the direction his thoughts were taking so refused to think on it any further. Instead he said, "Will you please just inform him that it is Colwyn Campbell. I would never disturb him at this time if it weren't a matter of the utmost importance. Once you inform him I am here, I really believe he'll change his mind and consent to see me."

Colwyn hoped the manservant would soften from his determination and the conviction in his voice and inform his master of their visit. It worked.

"Very well," the manservant finally relented, "I'll inform Lord Buchanan of your arrival but I cannot guarantee he'll grant you an audience. In the meantime, wait for my return here in the hall."

"Thank you," Colwyn uttered his appreciation.

The manservant turned to leave, but Colwyn had to find out, so he interrupted his departure by asking, "Before you go, may I ask for whom the house is in mourning?"

"The master's daughter, Miss Felicia, sir," the manservant turned and answered stiffly. "He just buried her several days past."

So it was true, Felicia was dead. Even though he had suspected it, Colwyn was still stunned by the confirmation of the news. His heart felt as if it had fallen to the bottom of his feet. This was not due to sorrow over the loss of Felicia, but from the tragedy he seemed to encounter at every avenue he crossed to retrieve the woman who owned his heart. He couldn't help asking himself, *Is everything for naught now? Would Lysette be denied to me forever?*

"But . . . but, how and why?" Colwyn uttered almost incoherently because this last revelation was almost his undoing.

"I'm afraid I'm not allowed to discuss the circumstances of this family's business with outsiders, sir."

The manservant is definitely an iceberg, thought Colwyn.

"So if you'll refrain from asking anything else, I'll be able to go and check with Lord Buchanan," the manservant retorted. This time he left unheeded.

Colwyn tried to get a grip on himself after this unexpected turn of events. He couldn't help but ask himself if Felicia's death now meant everything that had gone on before was all in vain? Then he bowed his head in hopeless despair. Never had fate dealt so many cards against him and he wondered if things could get any worse.

Ian noticed Colwyn's dejected state and hated to see him so despondent. "Don't give up the ship yet, young man, this unfortunate piece of news doesn't mean everything is hopeless." He laid his hand on Colwyn's shoulder in a comforting manner as he continued, "This might be a blessing in disguise. All I need is to get my hands on her spell book. From it I'm sure I can find the counter spell. She must have it hidden somewhere around here. If only we could gain some time in order to have a look see."

Immediately Colwyn perked up at hearing what Ian was saying. "Alexander might still give it to us. That is if he hasn't already had it burned. He was quite repulsed when he learned of Felicia's practices."

"Then pray as if the devil is nipping at your heels; that he hasn't had the time to do so yet," Ian responded optimistically.

Just then they heard the manservant returning and turned toward the footsteps expectantly.

"The master has consented to see you but only for a few moments. But only you," he addressed himself to Colwyn. "Your friend will have to wait in the sitting room. You may proceed while I show the gentleman where he is to wait."

Colwyn needed no second urging in heading down the long hallway to Alexander's study. Ian shouted at his retreating back, "Good luck, son! See you in a little while."

Alexander looks like death himself, was Colwyn's thought at his first glimpse of his old friend in just a matter of days. *What a change from his normally robust self. He looks as if he has aged a decade.* Drawing nearer to his friend, Colwyn suddenly found himself at a loss for words as he had felt no love for Felicia and after all the pain she had caused him, could not now mourn her loss. As it turned out, Alexander saved him the trouble by speaking first.

"Oh, Colwyn, it's my fault entirely, you know," Alexander reflected dejectedly.

Colwyn could see by the look of him that he was letting the guilt eat away at him.

"I should have been a more attentive father instead of spoiling her atrociously and letting her have her way in everything. But it was so much easier than dealing with her tantrums. If I had only applied a little discipline maybe this tragedy could have been avoided."

Privately Colwyn agreed with him but didn't voice his thoughts out loud for as soon as Alexander had finished saying that, he broke out in heart-rending sobs. Stunned for a moment, Colwyn didn't quite know how to go about comforting the man. Then he sighed and walked over to where Alexander was sitting and enfolded him in a sympathetic embrace.

How ironic, thought Colwyn. *Just a few moments ago*

I was the one who needed comforting. Now I'm the one giving it.

"You did what you thought best at the time, Alexander," Colwyn offered up these comforting words. "It simply makes no sense torturing yourself over it now. I do know one thing for sure; Felicia loved you with all her heart. On many occasions she told me so."

Actually, Felicia had done no such thing. Colwyn was convinced she loved no one except herself but couldn't see where this one little lie could hurt, especially if it brought a little comfort to an old man's grieving heart.

"Did she really speak of me to you?" Alexander asked, rousing himself a little from his grief to ask expectantly. He had trouble believing his totally selfish daughter had actually spoken of him.

"Yes, she did, all the time," Colwyn assured him.

Alexander pulled himself from Colwyn's embrace, now feeling slightly embarrassed by his display of emotion. "Listen to me carrying on this way about my problems," he offered as an apology. "Please forgive me for my negligence in my duties. What has brought you to visit and is it anything I can do for you? I know you couldn't have known of Felicia's death for I have informed no one outside the family. My reasons are purely selfish. In my deep shame over what she did, I feared it would be revealed to the entire community and this family would face the worst scandal it has ever been up against if the circumstances surrounding her death ever became known."

Colwyn had to know and said, "May I ask how she died? That is unless it pains you to speak of it."

"No, no. I don't mind telling you. I know I can trust you to never let the secret out. I feel I owe you so much more than that for all she has done to you."

"Alexander, I won't have you feeling that way," Colwyn stated forcefully. "You should know I could never blame you for what happened," he offered sincerely.

"Thank you for that, Colwyn. That's awfully kind of you but I can't help but blame myself. That maid of hers, Elsbeth, the witch, is the very one who got her started in all those black magic practices. She went up to Felicia's room the morning after you left here as usual to help Felicia rise. What she found was the most horrifying sight I've ever witnessed! For lying on the bed was not my cherished Felicia, but a pile of burnt bones and ashes."

"My god! No!" Colwyn exclaimed. "Are you certain it was her?"

"It was she. I have no doubt of that. I was hoping against hope it wasn't true but it was all in vain. My beautiful daughter is gone." Alexander sounded so empty and bereft to Colwyn.

"Do you know how the fire was started?" he then asked. "Was it an accident or do you think someone set it deliberately? I just can't see Felicia ever doing anything to harm herself," he said this thought out loud forgetting how insensitive it might sound to a grieving father.

Alexander seemed not to pay attention to it though, as he went on to further describe the scene. "It wasn't like anything I have ever seen before. It was not a normal fire because nothing else was burnt in her room except her and the bed sheet where she had lain, outlining her body. I still can't understand how it happened. It was if she burned from the inside out. It makes absolutely no sense."

Colwyn did not know what to make of this information but he felt certain it had to do with her practice of witchcraft. He would love to examine her remains but in order to do that they would have to exhume her body and he would hate to put Alexander through any more sorrow.

"Alexander, you know if there is anything I or my father can do, all you have to do is let us know. We'll be here in the blink of an eye."

"I thank you again, son, but for now all I want is for you to never reveal what you know about my Felicia. When her death is made known, I don't want her name besmirched. I know it's a lot to ask—to never reveal the truth, but it would mean so much to me."

"My father will have to know, but you can trust he will never utter a word."

"Yes, I know my old friend will keep the secret. I appreciate your thoughtfulness in this matter, Colwyn."

"It's the least we can do in the name of our friendship," Colwyn assured him.

"Now, we need to get to the reason for your visit," Alexander seemed anxious to change the subject.

"Well, then," Colwyn started off by saying, "I think we may have found a way to bring Lysette back home. The only problem is, I need your permission to access Felicia's spell book. The spell she used on Lysette may be in there and we're going to need it if we're going to counteract it."

"You found Ian then, and he can help?" Alexander sounded excited at the prospect.

"Yes, sir, I did and I believe he can help. As a matter of fact, he's waiting for me in your sitting room."

"Oh, Colwyn, I'm so glad for you, but I don't know if giving my permission is going to do you any good, for I don't know if it is here any longer," Alexander's excitement quickly changed to sorrowful regret. "I sent that witch, Elsbeth, packing early this morning as I could no longer stand the sight of her. I ordered her to take all that evil crap from my home for I wanted no reminders. I'm afraid she might already be gone because I haven't seen her since then."

Colwyn felt the desperation choking him up again but he had to try. There was just no giving up at this point. He asked, "Alexander, might I search that room just in case the book might still be there?"

"Why, yes, of course you may. Go have a look. And Colwyn, good luck, I hope you find it."

"Thank you. Let's pray luck is with me, for I feel I'm going to need it," Colwyn tossed back as he quickly dashed out the door to go and rejoin Ian and tell him the news.

As it turned out, luck was with him. When he and Ian entered the secret room, they found Elsbeth packing up her last few remaining items.

"Colwyn! Why have you returned here now?" Elsbeth shrieked after she glanced up and noticed them standing just inside the doorway. "If you've come to torture my Felicia, again, then you're too late. She's gone and you can never hurt her again."

"I haven't come looking for Felicia this time, Elsbeth. It's you I've come for," Colwyn calmly informed her.

"Oh, no!" Elsbeth responded frantically. "You'll get nothing out of me for I'm not afraid of the likes of ye. Haven't I suffered enough already? I've just recently lost the only person in the world I've ever really loved. She was like me own daughter. So there's nothing more you can do to me now to make me hurt even worse than I do already. So I dare ye to take your best shot."

"Save the false bravado for another time Elsbeth." Colwyn showed he was not impressed by her little speech. "I'm not interested in punishing you any further. I just want something I know you have. I want the book in which is written the spell Felicia used to send Lysette away."

"Why should I give it to ye?" Elsbeth sneered. "You're the very one that caused my Felicia such misery when you refused to love her."

"Because if you don't hand it over," Colwyn sneered ominously as he stepped in closer to Elsbeth, "I'll be tempted to break that hideously huge neck of yours."

Elsbeth inched away from his threatening stance and apparently thought her decision over at least twice when she read the seriousness in his gleaming, determined eyes. She actually believed he would enjoy doing just what he said and reached into the bag she had strapped over her shoulder and pulled out the book.

"Here it is, you bastard," she cursed as she practically threw it at him. "Now leave me alone for I never want to set eyes on ye again!"

"Just one minute, Elsbeth," Colwyn warned. "I need to know the spell she used and no tricks either," he warned. "For if I find out you have lied to me, I will hunt you down like the dog you are, slice you up, and separate your pieces to the far corners of the earth—"

Elisabeth's eyes widened in horror as she saw the truth of his vow in his eyes and all her hopes of revenge went up in smoke just as had her beloved Felicia.

"It is on page 136," Elsbeth answered truthfully but with reluctance. "I hope it don't do you much good!" she shouted at his disappearing form through the doorway. "You never deserved her love! She was much too good for the likes of you!"

Colwyn found himself wondering just who she meant, Felicia or Lysette. Then he began to realize just where Felicia had gotten most of her nastiness.

16

THE TWO MEN HURRIED BACK to Castle Campbell as fast as they could because Colwyn was eager for Ian to get started studying the spell as soon as possible. Earlier he had directed one of the up-stairs servants to prepare a room for Ian so since it was ready, he then accompanied Ian to the room himself. "Is the room suitable, Ian?" he asked.

Ian replied, "Seems very comfortable indeed, but I want no interruptions until I emerge from the room. It will take all my powers of concentration to see and follow each of Felicia's steps before I will be able to figure out how to counteract her spell and hopefully bring Lysette back."

Immediately upon Colwyn's leaving the room and the door closing behind him, Ian began to diligently study the spell. Going through the castle, Colwyn ordered the staff not to disturb their guest for any reason. He told them, "If anyone is caught near his door, making any noise, there will be a serious reprimand; maybe even a termination of employment!" Colwyn had never been that harsh with the family servants before but then again he had never encountered a problem such as this and his servants understood his behavior. Not a one dared to disregard his instructions.

After what seemed like hours to Colwyn but in reality was only a brief time, Ian came out looking like a different man all together. Before tackling the spell, he had taken the time to bathe, shave and comb his overly long, shabby hair. His clothes had been cleaned and actually fit rather nicely on him. He looked quite presentable and Colwyn couldn't help but comment upon his changed appearance, laying eyes on him for the first time in several hours. "Hey, old man . . . you clean up almost respectably. I had to take a second look just to make sure it was really you."

Ian broke out with a broad grin at Colwyn's backhanded compliment and seemed a little embarrassed at his easy familiarity but shrugged it off as he approached Colwyn. "It is as I suspected," he commented, his conclusions going straight to the business at hand. "She used a time-transference spell to transport Lysette. If I am to send you to her, we'll need several things to accomplish it."

"Name them and they're yours," Colwyn promised.

"First of all," Ian continued, "I'll need to know what area she was in when she disappeared."

"That shouldn't present a problem. Jeremy will be able to tell us that because he witnessed the event as it was happening," replied Colwyn.

"The next request might be a little more difficult to fulfill," Ian predicted. "We'll need five more people, besides you and I, who are willing to believe. And I mean *really* believe Colwyn, for I'll need their absolute concentration for this thing to work."

"Don't worry," Colwyn declared. "Somehow, we'll find them."

"Since I'll need the help of a more powerful force to send you through time, I'm going to conduct what is known as a séance," Ian explained.

Colwyn had heard of séances before and of the people

who conducted them but had never put much faith in the practice. Now as he listened to Ian's explanation as to how he would perform it and what he expected the end result to be, Colwyn found himself hoping against hope that it would be as Ian said would take place. Suddenly he felt a renewed strength flow through him.

"I'm positive my father will be eager to participate," Colwyn assured him with confidence in his voice. "There's also Lysette's father. Hopefully he's not too ill to be a part of it. Her disappearance has just about undone him. Of course Jeremy and Mac will be there for us. And last, but certainly not least, there's Lysette's maid, Amy. She'd never forgive us if we didn't include her."

"Good," Ian muttered, "we must get prepared. The séance will have to be performed very near to where Jeremy saw her last standing for you to be able to appear in the same area where she was sent. You go and gather up our participants while I gather up the items for the ceremony," Ian told Colwyn. "I'll give you the last of the details when you return. . . ."

Colwyn was out the door almost before Ian had finished speaking but returned in practically no time with his believers who were ready and even eager to help. Asa Duncan showed the first signs of real life since his daughter's disappearance after Colwyn explained the situation to him. He was eager to try anything if it might mean Lysette's safe return.

They all proceeded out to the gardens where Jeremy showed Ian the exact location from where Lysette disappeared. Then Ian took it from there telling them, "It must be very dark where we hold the séance as it is very important that no light slip through and we must join hands while forming a circle. So where is the best place where we can accomplish this feat?" he asked.

"The library is just through those doors," Colwyn indicated "and it is very dark."

"Excellent!" Ian exclaimed. "Then we will need a round table and seven chairs."

"There's already a table and some chairs in there," Colwyn informed him. "The table has been used for studying but I believe we can round up seven chairs to encircle it."

"Well then, let's go give this thing a try," Ian stated optimistically as the rest of the group gathered quickly in the room.

After everything had been made ready to Ian's specifications, he stood ready to begin. Seated in the chairs, the eyes of the six chosen people stared intently as Ian prepared to speak.

"Colwyn," he addressed him exclusively at first, "there are a few more things I must tell you before we proceed. They are very important, so listen closely. As I've already told you, Lysette needs to remember you before I can bring her back. Also, she must believe in the power or I can do nothing for her. Another thing, she has to realize and accept she is in the wrong time. I don't care how you do it; just make her remember. Even if it is the most drastic thing you've ever done.

"Another thing, don't be alarmed at all the strange things you'll encounter as it might draw attention to you and make the people of that period very suspicious. Just act like everything is perfectly familiar to you. Remember, they live in a far more advanced civilization than ours.

"Next, and this is the most important thing of all, you *must* bring her back to the place where you first appear before mid-night. If you fail to do so, you will be stuck in that time period forever as I won't be able to hold the portal open any longer than that."

"Good god, Ian," Colwyn exclaimed, "why not leave the best for last next time!"

Colwyn was clearly upset at hearing that last bit of information and said, "You're not giving me very much time to accomplish this miracle."

"I'm sorry, my boy," Ian sincerely apologized. "I should have told you sooner but I didn't want to dampen your spirits. If you're too worried and stressed this might not work. You have to be in the best frame of mind as possible."

"I'm sorry also, Ian. I shouldn't have been so sarcastic and disrespectful and barked at you like that. I am too weary from lack of sleep but I shouldn't take it out on you. Truly, I am grateful you decided to help me and I appreciate everything you have done so far."

"Forget it, son, as I don't hold it against you. I'm not offended by your outburst and can certainly understand your feelings. We'll just put it behind us. Agreed?"

"Agreed," Colwyn said shaking Ian's hand.

Then Ian asked everyone to join hands, as he snuffed out the candles and darkness filled the room. Soon he began some strange mutterings in an unrecognizable tongue. Every head was bent; every eye closed in an unfailing belief in miracles. Colwyn prayed silently to the Lord, that he would find Lysette very soon.

Suddenly there was a loud thunderclap as a flash of bright light flooded the room. It happened so quickly no one was quite sure what he or she saw. Ian lit the lamps and all were thunderstruck as they glanced about the table and realized Colwyn was no longer seated with them.

17

Summer 2005

Edinburgh, Scotland

BEING LEFT ALONE IN THE apartment for most of the day, Lysette found she was becoming restless and bored. There was only so much television one could watch without feeling burned out. (She was beginning to pick up their colorful phrases.) Today, though, she was experiencing a little excitement as this morning before leaving for work, the girls had confessed they had a little surprise in store for her that night. She hoped it meant getting out of the apartment for a little while because she desperately needed a change of scenery. As the walls seemed to be closing in on her after staring at them for so long, she eagerly awaited their arrival back at the apartment.

Lorna, Stacy, and Susan were talking about that just as they were getting ready to leave the office that afternoon.

"I don't know, Lorna," Stacy replied. "Do you think it's safe to take Lisa to a place like the Paddy Wagon? I mean, I'd lay 100 to 1 odds she's never been exposed to such an atmosphere."

"She'll be with us," Lorna answered. "I believe she'll be just fine as long as we stick close by her."

"I suppose so," Stacy agreed.

"Lorna, don't you think it's a bit odd that we haven't heard about any inquires concerning her yet? I mean, it's been almost two weeks. Someone should be looking for her by now. After all, she was wearing the most exquisite wedding gown I've ever laid eyes on. I haven't seen a period piece like that since . . . well, hell; I've never seen anything like that! Nobody puts that much hand work in them anymore."

"I know, Stacy," Lorna responded, "and I can't say I haven't been a little worried about the whole situation. But right now, all we can do is be there for her and wait."

"Don't get me wrong. I like Lisa a lot," Stacy continued, "and I really enjoy her staying with us, but I have to mention this, because the thought did occur to me, even though I hate myself for thinking it. Do you think she could be some escaped loony from a mental hospital?" Stacy held her breath waiting for an answer.

"She seems perfectly sane to me," Lorna answered quite calmly, not displaying any surprise or disgust at Stacy's question as she had been expecting it, "despite the fact she still can't remember very much about herself. Besides, I'm a little ashamed to admit it now, after coming to know and like her as much as I do, that I'd already thought of that scenario and had checked out all the local mental facilities. No one answering her description has ever been treated in any of them, much less escaped from a place like that. Come to think of it, how would you figure she could ever get her hands on a dress like that if she'd been institutionalized?"

"You've got a good point there, Lorna," Stacy surmised. "Let's change the subject and talk about tonight's events."

"Agreed," they replied in unison.

“Who did Rick get to come tonight to be with Lisa and make up the number?” Lorna then asked Stacy.

“A friend of his by the name of Jerry,” she answered. “He hasn’t known him very long and I’ve never met him, but Rick says he’s okay, so I’ll trust his word.” Then she addressed her other friend saying, “Susan, are you sure you and Brad wouldn’t like to join us this evening?”

“I’m positive, Stacy,” Susan answered. “Tonight is just not a good night. I really must stay home and study for the bar exam.”

“Oh, come on, now,” Stacy urged, “one Friday night isn’t going to hurt.”

“Maybe not, but it won’t be tonight,” Susan countered.

“Oh, all right, I give up,” Stacy grudgingly said. “You’re just like an unmovable boulder. Go ahead and stay at home with your boring books while the rest of us go out and have the time of our lives.”

Turning to Lorna, Stacy replied, “Let’s hurry home. I’m really beginning to look forward to this evening.”

The girls arrived home in a flurry of excitement and soon Lysette got caught up in their bubbling banter. They had told her they would like to eat early tonight so they could have more time to get ready. Therefore, she already had supper spread out on the table for them. It was a simple fare of pasta and salad but Lysette found she enjoyed cooking in the quite convenient kitchen.

At first she had been slightly amazed at all the handy appliances when the girls had first shown them to her. They practically did everything themselves, thus requiring little effort on her part. Quickly she had caught on though, and had whipped up a very appetizing delight for that night. The girls thought they were in heaven as they feasted and thoroughly appreciated her thoughtfulness.

Lorna's boyfriend, Steve, called while they were finishing up and informed her they would pick them up around 8:30 P.M. She hung up the phone in the bathroom then said with an impish grin, "I think we should give the works to Lisa first. Don't you Stacy?"

"Most definitely," Stacy answered. "Her make-over shouldn't take too long since she's a natural beauty anyway."

Her compliment held a touch of envy in it even though it was given good-naturedly. Lysette thanked her for her praise a little shyly with a faint blush.

"Have a seat on the toilet lid, Lisa," Lorna told her indicating the object with a wave of her hand. "Sorry we don't have a vanity table, but this bathroom is much too small to accommodate one."

"That's all right, Lorna," Lysette replied. "I don't mind sitting here. Actually, I find it quite comfortable and rather handy. You know where I come from, we have to use chamber pots."

Lorna dropped the brush she was about to stroke through Lysette's hair and exclaimed, "You don't mean to say you actually remember using one of those things, do you?"

Lysette looked stunned for a moment before she replied, "Well, yes, I guess I do!"

Lorna got really excited at hearing this saying, "Lisa, do you realize what that means? You've just had your first of many memories return. Now we really have a good reason to celebrate."

Her delight was infectious to Lysette, but Stacy just looked thoughtful for a moment before she asked, "You mean to tell me Lisa just had her first memory return and it was of using a chamber pot?"

The three just looked at each other in silence for a few seconds then burst out in uncontrollable laughter.

"What a memory to have return!" Lorna managed to sputter out through her guffaws, as she wiped the tears from her eyes. "I haven't laughed this hard in ages." She then continued, "But now it's time to get serious again and finish up with this beautiful lady. She must look stunning tonight."

"That shouldn't be too hard as she's practically already there," Stacy chimed in.

"Don't you know it!" Lorna agreed. "Her hair is absolutely glorious," she sighed enviously. "I've always wanted hair that was thick and naturally curly."

"Oh, no, you shouldn't think that way, Lorna. Your hair is very beautiful straight. It suits you very well," Lysette piped up to assure her.

"Thank you, Lisa, but I think you are just being kind" Lorna beamed.

"Oh, no, I really mean it! You look gorgeous just the way you are." Lysette seemed anxious to convince her.

"All right, all right, I believe you," Lorna reassured her. "Now, I think your hair would look lovely up, with little curling tendrils around your heart shaped face."

"You know, what you're doing to my hair, reminds me of other times," Lysette reflected.

"Really! What?" the two surprised friends uttered in unison.

"I'm seeing the image of a very buxom woman," Lysette told them. "A woman I somehow feel is very close to me. She's bustling around me like a mother hen, doing up my hair in the same fashion as you're now doing."

"That's great, Lisa. I believe we're having a major break-through here!" Lorna exclaimed. "See, I told you your memories could come flooding back at any time. But don't try to concentrate too hard. It could do more harm than good and you could end up with one excruciating headache."

"I'll try not to but it's all so exciting," Lysette promised.

"Well, right now all I want you to think about is how much fun we're going to have tonight!" Lorna ordered good-naturedly.

"Now, Stacy," Lorna said as she turned to her companion, "I need your opinion here since you're the expert. What cosmetics do you think we should use to bring out her coloring?"

"I think the violet-rose combination should do very nicely but not a whole lot." Stacy answered. "It won't take very much with eyes the color of hers. I declare, they could rival Elizabeth Taylor's."

"Who is Elizabeth Taylor?" Lysette piped up. "Is she a friend of yours also?"

"Goodness!" Stacy exclaimed. "If you've never heard of Elizabeth Taylor, you have really been cut off from society."

"That's not important right now," Lorna declared. "What is important is getting finished up here. We have not one, but two reasons now to celebrate."

If you count my recurring dream every night of the mysteriously handsome man who swept me off my feet and tantalized my senses, then there would be three reasons to celebrate, Lysette thought to herself but didn't feel quite ready to share that information with anyone else yet because she still hadn't decided if it had been an actual event in her life or merely a fabrication of her mind.

The men were true to their word as the apartment's doorbell rang at precisely 8:29 P.M. Lorna opened the door to their smiling faces. Steve, Rick, and Jerry stood there looking handsome and well groomed in their shirts and slacks. She ushered them in and introduced Lysette to her date.

She looked smashing in her somewhat low-cut, off-white satin blouse, black leather mini-skirt and matching black leather boots. Her stockings were natural, to blend with her fair skin. Lorna had lent Lysette her pearls that complemented the outfit.

Personally, Lysette had a feeling she had never worn anything so daring before. She didn't know how she knew it, but she felt certain of that fact.

Jerry was certainly pleased at what he saw when first being introduced to Lysette as was evident by the big grin spread across his face.

Rick had explained Lysette's situation to him from what Stacy had imparted. Since this was not to be an official date, he was just to act as a companion, tonight, so as not to have an awkward number and leave Lysette feeling left out. After first setting eyes on her though, Jerry hoped to change that situation and get to know her a lot better. He thought to himself, *And to think I almost declined, for I thought it would be a bummer night. When I finally accepted, I did so on the condition Rick would owe me big time. Now I'll have to remember to thank him!*

Lysette's first impression of Jerry was slightly different. Though he was certainly handsome enough, she didn't feel any "sparks." Instead, she felt a little uneasy, in a way she couldn't explain. *Maybe it is just nervousness at the upcoming evening and not anything directed at him,* she told herself.

He was of average height, with slightly long blonde hair and aqua-blue eyes. What he lacked in height though, he obviously made up for in build. She could detect his bulging muscles even through his jacket. All in all, she thought his eyes were his best features even though she suspected there was something lacking in them. He presented a friendly facade but she decided she would reserve her judgment till later on as the evening progressed.

After the introductions were made and the usual formalities were out of the way, Lorna suggested they be on their way.

When they arrived, The Paddy Wagon was really rocking that night, if the loud blaring music coming through the door was any indication. As they inched their way through the crowded entrance, Lysette exclaimed in alarm, "Oh, my god, I believe this place is on fire! We'll have to leave at once."

The men looked puzzled at her remark but Lorna knew instantly to what she was referring and hurried to explain. "You don't have to worry about that, Lisa. It's perfectly normal for it to be this smoky. It comes from all the cigarettes being smoked at once from many different people. You'll get used to it after a while."

Lysette highly doubted it as she swept her hands back and forth to clear the air in front of her face and gave Lorna a look of disbelief. She didn't see how anyone could get used to not being able to freely breathe.

They finally made their way in, and lucky for them, Rick had had the foresight to reserve a table; otherwise they wouldn't have been able to find one. He gave his name to the hostess and she showed them to their table. After the ladies were seated, a waitress asked for their drink order. It was beer all around except for Lysette who hadn't acquired a taste for the bitter brew. Instead, she asked for a glass of white wine.

They had only been there a few short minutes before Jerry asked Lysette to dance. Glancing up at all the gyrating people on the crowded dance floor she mischievously remarked, "Is that what they're doing up there? I thought all those people were in serious pain."

The entire group cracked up at her remark.

"I'm not sure I would be able to move like that," she confessed to Jerry.

"Oh sure you can," he told her. "It's really fun and easy once you give it a try. Or if you prefer, we could wait for a slow one."

He was hoping she would choose the later, as he really wanted to feel her full breasts pressed close against him. Lysette noted the lascivious gaze in his eyes and chose the first offer. She didn't feel she wanted to be that close to Jerry. "I've decided to give that a try," she told him, indicating the dance floor.

Jerry was a little disappointed at her choice, but decided not to let it show. Putting on a cheerful face, he said as he stood up and pulled out Lysette's chair, "Good, I'm glad you relented. Let's go give this thing a whirl."

She smiled at his remark but couldn't help the queer feeling of apprehension that settled in the pit of her stomach. *I hope I won't feel this way for the rest of the evening,* she told herself.

18

Summer 2005

Edinburgh, Scotland

COLWYN SLOWLY REGAINED HIS SENSE of awareness after he materialized in unfamiliar surroundings. Traveling through time had to be one of the strangest sensations one could ever experience. Little had Colwyn known that when he had told Lysette he would search for her in every time and go anyplace to find her, that he would be transported 300 years into the future to do so.

Looking around, he took note of the area and realized he was standing in what looked to be a chapel. In amazement he said to himself, *So this is now where my castle once stood?* He found it hard to imagine that majestic building as being gone but took comfort in the fact that if it had to be anything but his home, he was glad it had become a church.

Hearing a noise just off to his left, a short distance ahead that sounded to him like a door being opened, he jerked his head in that direction.

Reverend Morgan was just stepping out of his office as he had been going over his notes for next Sunday's sermon before he decided to head for home. He noticed the young man standing in the middle of the chapel, looking quite perplexed and in a friendly manner greeted him,

“Hello there, young sir, I’m Reverend Morgan, may I help you with something?”

Colwyn was certainly glad to be met by this personable man of God. For some reason, he had a strong feeling this man could help him with Lysette’s whereabouts. He answered, “I certainly hope so. Perhaps you could help me with the location of my missing fiancée. She’s an extraordinarily lovely young woman who was wearing an exquisite wedding gown. Is there any chance you might have seen anyone like that?”

The reverend beamed a big wide grin at hearing that. He was glad someone had finally showed up to give that sweet young miss an identity. She’d been waiting anxiously for at least a couple of weeks now.

“I’d be happy to help,” the Reverend replied. “I know of the lady to whom you are referring. She’s now one of my members.”

Colwyn could feel the excitement bubbling up in his bloodstream at this news and blurted out, “Is she here then?”

“I’m sorry to quell your enthusiasm but, no,” the Reverend answered. “Though I do know where she is staying. She’s with some very nice young ladies who are also church members here.”

“Will you take me to her?” Colwyn asked hopefully.

“Of course I will. They’ll all be glad to finally meet you. I’m afraid we were all beginning to believe the little thing didn’t have a soul in her life claiming to know her. Before we leave though, I must ask you if you are aware she has lost her memory?”

Colwyn suddenly found it hard to determine just how much to reveal to the Reverend. After all, this day and age was a far more advanced civilization than his, which was 300 years after his time. He had no way of knowing if time travel was a commonplace happening to them so decided at this point it would be better to keep his information to a minimum.

"Yes, I'm aware of that fact," Colwyn answered. "I'm hoping I can get her to remember me."

"Well, I wish you luck and answered prayers," the Reverend enthused. "If you don't mind my asking, son, could you tell me what happened to her and why it took you so long to show up?"

"I wish I could Reverend," *May God forgive me for this lie,* "but I'm not really sure myself. And the reason it took me this long is because I've just now been able to find her. I can tell you this though; I love her with every bit of my being and would never do anything to cause her any harm if that puts your mind at ease."

Being convinced, Reverend Morgan said, "I gather you must've been out of the area and a great distance away to get here as soon as you learned of her whereabouts," the reverend remarked.

Colwyn was a little puzzled at this comment and said, "I beg your pardon?" He wasn't sure how the reverend had guessed he had traveled such a great distance.

"Forgive me," the reverend excused. "I meant no insult or disrespect. It is just that your kilt is a little disheveled, almost as if you might have slept in it. The Campbell's colors and patterns on your tartan look barely distinguishable."

Colwyn looked down at himself and was faced with the truth of the reverend's statement. Immediately he felt shame at entering the Lord's holy chapel in such a shabby state of dress.

"I'm very sorry, Reverend. I wasn't thinking. I mean no disrespect to this holiest of places."

"That's quite all right. No need to apologize," the reverend reassured him. "I perfectly understand your situation."

"I take it from your statement before that you are familiar with the tartan of the Campbell's," Colwyn quizzed a little surprised.

"I should hope so!" the reverend boomed proudly. "It was the Campbells who donated all this land to the church. Actually, it was an earl from the eighteenth century I believe. His name was Colwyn Campbell. His Campbell descendants live close by on one of the most beautiful estates in the city. They're my most faithful members."

Colwyn's mouth dropped open in amazement then said, "Reverend, you must forgive me my late manners in not introducing myself earlier. My name also is Colwyn Campbell," and he reached out to shake the reverend's hand.

The reverend grasped it readily in acceptance and commented, "My, word, this is remarkable. You must be related. It is a great pleasure to meet you. Were you named for the Earl then?" he asked enthusiastically.

"You could say that," Colwyn quirked humorously at the irony. "Although the relation is quite distant," Colwyn coughed a little to hide his humor. "I haven't had the pleasure of meeting my relatives in this area. . . . I'm afraid I've never had the time."

The reverend thought this odd, but did not comment. Instead he sympathized saying, "I'm sorry to hear that as they are wonderful people. We'll have to remedy that situation as soon as possible."

"It will have to be later, Reverend, but thank you," Colwyn told him. "Right now I am in quite a hurry to get to Lysette."

"Of course, we'll see to that at once." The reverend

had understood perfectly as he shook his head in agreement.

That would be something, Colwyn thought to himself, *to actually tell your children that you met their children's, children's, children, and so forth.*

"Would you like to change before we proceed? I thought you might like to freshen up a bit, to feel a little better," the reverend kindly suggested.

"That's very thoughtful of you, reverend. Even though I'm very anxious to get to Lysette, I wouldn't want to be too conspicuous in a crowd or offend anyone with the stench of this outfit."

Colwyn found himself wondering just what the clothes the reverend wanted to lend him would look like.

"I would love to change. Do you have anything that will fit? I am of a rather large size," he stated rather obviously.

"I believe I just may have," the reverend remarked. "There are some used clothes in my office that are still in good condition. A few of my parishioners have donated them for the needy. I believe there may be some that will fit you. Would you like to take a look see and borrow some for a little while?"

"I would appreciate that very much, Reverend. Thank you."

Colwyn found he wanted to blend in and feel clean and comfortable again.

"Glad to be of service," the reverend replied. "Let's just dash in there and see what we can find."

Quickly the reverend found a cotton-polyester blend shirt and a pair of denim jeans that appeared to be close to Colwyn's size. "Here," he said, handing the clothes over to Colwyn. "These should be a close enough fit. You may take them to the men's room just down the hall, second door to the left and try them on in there. Don't worry about returning them right away if they fit. You can just bring them back when you return for your own clothes. I'll have them washed and dried for you."

Colwyn smiled as he appreciated the effort Reverend Morgan was going through to help him, but he hoped he wasn't here long enough to come back and retrieve his clean clothes. He just nodded his assent as he followed the reverend's directions to the men's room. Though he had no idea what the "men's room" was, he was certainly on his way there. Upon entering, to him it was definitely an odd looking room. Upon taking a quick look around, he noted there were several strange looking objects attached to the far wall and a few enclosures to the side further down which made him wonder what was in there.

Actually, he didn't know what to make of the room, so he decided to examine the clothes in his arms. He figured they shouldn't be too difficult to get on and began to undress. The shirt was a jade-green color, just a shade darker than his eyes. Though the material felt soft, the fit was rather snug around his chest and arms because of his muscular build but he noted it complemented his color rather nicely. The collar opened up into a deep V-cut, exposing the springy soft curly hairs of his chest. What rather amazed him though were the pants and he remembered the reverend had called them "denim jeans." This material also was soft to the touch and quite comfortable once he pulled them on. But he could also tell they were quite durable and figured they'd be good pants in which to work. The thought crossed his mind that it would be nice if he could take them back with him to his time.

Reverend Morgan was waiting for his return as he emerged from the men's room and commented, "I see they're a little tight but they'll be all right for now. Don't you think?"

Colwyn looked down at himself, nodded and said, "Yes, I suppose so," as he noted that his thighs were molded and outlined in this strange new material and they brushed against one another with a swishing sound as he walked.

"Fine," the reverend commented at Colwyn's acceptance. "Are you ready now to retrieve your lady-love?"

Colwyn sighed with the sound of satisfied anticipation and confided, "More ready than you'll ever know, Reverend."

* * *

Oh, no, not now, of all times! Susan thought irritably of the insistent knocking that intruded upon her studying. For half-a-second she seriously considered ignoring the summons, but by the sound knew that whoever was on the other side was not about to give up that easily. *Damn, and just when I almost had this thing down pat. Oh, well, I might as well go answer the door now and quickly get it over with so I can get back to my studies.*

She jerked the door open rather roughly in her annoyance, and immediately felt shame-faced as she stood face to face with Reverend Morgan.

"Reverend," she muttered a little embarrassed, "how nice to see you. Come in. Can I help you with something? I'm afraid we weren't expecting you this evening."

"I'm glad you're here, Susan," the reverend greeted her cheerily. "We thought for a moment no one was at home."

She blushed guiltily at his remark and that was when she noticed he was not alone.

"Forgive my intruding, dear. I realize you were not expecting any visitors but I have with me someone I know you'll be glad to meet," indicating Colwyn at his side.

Susan glanced over to the reverend's right and her mouth fell open in awe. There standing before her was the most drop-dead gorgeous man she'd ever had the pleasure of encountering. His smile was so dazzling she felt it could rival the sunshine. *Hmm, she sighed inwardly, now why couldn't Brad look like that?*

"Susan, this is Mr. Colwyn Campbell," the reverend went on to introduce him. "He's looking for our lost little Lisa and claims to be her fiancé."

Pointing a hand at her he said, "Colwyn, this is Susan Howard, one of the fine young ladies who has taken in your fiancée."

Turning back to Susan he asked, "Does she happen to be in now, my dear?"

"Oh, my, God!" Susan exclaimed as she clasped her hands to her face. "This is wonderful! Am I ever glad to finally meet you," and she demonstrated by rushing up to Colwyn to grasp and shake his hand. "Lisa will be thrilled, to say the very least. It seems as if she's waited forever."

"Excuse me," Colwyn interjected pleasantly, "who is this 'Lisa' to whom you keep referring?"

"Oh, forgive me!" Susan exclaimed. "That's just what we call her. What is her real name?"

"Her name is Lysette Duncan," Colwyn said trying to hide his impatience, "and I'm very anxious to see her. Is she here then?" he said wanting to charge through the door.

"What a coincidence, we call her by something so close to her actual name. It's almost like ESP somehow.

Don't you think?" Susan didn't realize she was rattling on and on.

Colwyn was getting rather agitated by this time but he didn't want to be rude. He pointedly asked again, "Miss, please, can you tell me whether she's here or not?"

"Oh goodness, forgive me, I'm so sorry for going on like that," she apologized. "Actually, she isn't in at the moment. But I have a pretty good idea where she'd be at this time. I can take you there, if you'd like."

Colwyn was still further annoyed at yet another delay but tried not to show it. With a forced smile he said, "That would be wonderful, miss. May we leave right away?"

"Why, yes, of course. No problem," Susan answered. "And oh, by the way, please call me Susan. Miss sounds so formal."

"Thank you mis—I mean, Susan," he smiled at her.

Susan thought she'd died and gone to heaven when he looked at her that way. He could have asked her for anything in the world at that moment and she'd only have been too happy to comply. "That's quite all right," she beamed up at him. "Would you mind riding in my car? You see, I have to hurry back here to finish my studying."

Colwyn had not the slightest inkling as to what she was referring, but if giving her an affirmative answer meant getting to Lysette faster, he'd agree to anything. "That's fine by me," he gave by way of an answer.

"Good, we'll get rolling then," she threw back at him as she grabbed up her car keys from the end table.

The reverend chose this moment to make his presence felt again saying, "I'll have to be getting on home now. I'm afraid the missus will be wondering what's taking me so long. I'm usually home by now, snoring blissfully away in my easy chair. But I'll be wanting to wish you good luck and Godspeed, young man. I hope everything turns out for the best between the two of you."

Reverend Morgan knew there was much more to this young man's story than what little information he was giving them, but he was not one to pry into things that someone didn't yet want to talk about. And he definitely had the impression this particular young man didn't want to say anything more than what he needed. Maybe, some other time perhaps, when he felt like opening up.

"Thank you, Reverend. I appreciate all you've done for me so far. I just wish there was something I could do for you as well." Colwyn had never felt more sincere as he spoke these words to the reverend.

"Don't give it a second thought as it was my pleasure. I'm a great believer in happy endings. You drive safely now," he said, directing his words at Susan.

"I will . . . see you in church on Sunday," she piped up as he turned and walked away.

The reverend waved goodbye just before he rounded the corner in the hallway and slipped out of sight.

19

SUSAN LED COLWYN TO A COMPACT Mazda Miata that was in the parking lot outside their apartment building. She told him off-handedly, "I'll unlock your door first so you can climb in."

Colwyn stared in amazement at the object of her statement and loudly exclaimed, "You expect me to get in that!"

"Look, I realize you're an awfully large man, but I assure you you'll be able to fit. It's bigger than it looks. There's plenty of room in there," Susan told him, completely misunderstanding his meaning that it wasn't the size he was referring to, but the actual object itself.

He had seen these so-called horseless carriages whizzing past on the road while he and the reverend had walked over to the apartment. The girls didn't live too far from the church, so the reverend had suggested they walk as he enjoyed the exercise. Colwyn had to admit he was a bit fascinated with how they seemed to operate, but also was a little apprehensive about actually riding in one.

Susan stood there holding the car door open for him, looking quite expectant, so he had no other choice but to climb in. He watched her every move as she started the thing, backed up and maneuvered it out onto the road and into the traffic.

"Don't tell me you're already frightened of my driving? You've only been in here barely a minute," she joked as she looked at his shocked expression on his now ashen face. "We've hardly even begun to move and yet you're staring at me as if you expect to die any second now."

In fascination, he had totally forgotten his manners and at once apologized saying, "Forgive me. I didn't realize I was staring so intently. Your driving is fine by me. I meant no disrespect."

He had known how hard he had been staring but hadn't realized he was being observed as well.

"That's okay, I'll let you off this time," she laughingly joked at him to lighten his oh-so-serious mood. "Just relax, we'll be there in no time. It's not very far from here."

Colwyn tried to get comfortable by stretching out his legs a little but they were too long to maneuver in the limited space. Susan witnessed his dilemma and informed him there was a button on the right side, at the bottom of his seat that he could push down in order to move the seat back. He found it and did as she instructed and his eyes grew wide at the shock of his discovery and Susan witnessed this also. Her curiosity was about to bubble over so she decided to initiate a conversation in the small confines of the now awkward and silent car.

"Have you and Lis—I mean Lysette—known each other for very long?"

Colwyn really didn't feel like answering any questions because he was afraid of what he might reveal. But on the other hand realized he couldn't ignore her either. If it weren't for her kindness, he might never have been able to find Lysette in time. Instead of answering, he decided to ask one of his own. "Why do you ask that?"

She was taken a little off guard at his counter question, but decided to answer anyway. "It's just that neither of you seem to know about any modern conveniences. I thought it might be possible you grew up together in a sequestered community."

Colwyn thought it best to continue to let her think that way and answered, "Yes, that's exactly right. We grew up together."

He did not want to elaborate any further and Susan took the hint from the tone in his voice. She decided to alter the course of their conversation and commented, "You must have loved her a long time then."

"I feel as if I have loved her for centuries," Colwyn confessed, smiling a little after this last statement.

Susan just smiled and continued to drive in silence, taking a hint from his pensive mood. In what seemed to Colwyn just a few short moments later, Susan announced, "We're here. See, I told you it wouldn't take that long. And, hey, you're in one piece also. Now do you trust my driving?"

Colwyn didn't realize she was kidding with him so as to lighten the mood a little after her probing questions and answered rather seriously, "Of course, I trust you. Have my actions given you any reason to doubt it?"

"I see now we're going to have to work on your sense of humor," she retorted while giving him a pat on the arm.

After giving her an odd look she said, "Oh, come on, let's go in."

She gave up trying to explain and grabbed him by the arm and ushered him toward the door. He let her lead the way. Inside the building it was dark, crowded and smoke-filled. Making their way through the crowd the going was rather slow and he found himself getting slightly irritated as none of these people seemed to want to step out of the way. He just barely managed to hold onto Susan's hand as she maneuvered him through the masses.

All of a sudden she squealed out, causing him to jump

and jerk back around. "I see them! They're sitting over there at the table," she said pointing off in a further direction trying to show him where she meant.

Colwyn's heart did a flip-flop and started beating what felt like 300 beats per minute at the prospect of finally seeing Lysette once again. When he actually did lay eyes on her, he found it hard to believe she was positively the real thing and not some mirage his mind had conjured up to keep him from going insane. She was just as lovely as he had remembered, sitting as regally as a princess, even in this awful place, completely oblivious to his presence.

Before Susan could make another move or say another word, he bounded right over to her; seeing no one and forgetting everything except Lysette.

"Lysette, it is really you! Thank God, I've finally found you! It feels as if I've searched forever. But everything will soon be all right as long as we leave this place right now so I can get you back home."

At the sound of the strange man's voice directly in front of her, Lysette looked up and stared into the emerald green eyes of the most incredibly handsome man she could ever recall meeting. He was looking at her as if he couldn't quite believe what he was seeing and she had the strangest feeling she'd seen that penetrating gaze that seemed to probe into the deep recesses of her soul, somewhere before, but the image seemed to elude her.

"I beg your pardon, sir," she replied cool as a cucumber even though she was quaking inside, "Are you speaking to me?"

She became even more puzzled at his expression. Her companions were oddly quiet, staring with interest at the exchange between the two that appeared to electrify the atmosphere.

"Of course I'm speaking to you." His look seemed to imply she had taken leave of her senses. "And what in God's name are you doing dressed like that?"

Colwyn had completely forgotten about her absent memory in the thrill of seeing her again and in his heated jealousy, stemming from her appearance. Then it hit him like a ton of bricks and he sighed morosely. *How could I have been so indelicate?* he chastised himself.

Still, his realization didn't ease his distress any as he took note of his surroundings. He didn't like the fact Lysette was exposing so much flesh to other men's lustful gazes; especially the weasel-faced blonde sitting right next to her looking as if he could devour her at any minute.

"I don't believe that's any concern of yours, sir, and I'll thank you not to take that tone with me," Lysette commented in an offended manner in reference to Colwyn's latest remark. "And why do you refer to me as someone named 'Lysette'? I believe you have mistaken me for someone else."

Now this sounded more like the Lysette he remembered—completely obstinate and refusing to look into her heart and realize the truth.

"If you'd stop being so stubborn for only a moment, you'd know why and come home with me right now!" Colwyn practically shouted at her.

Though he knew Lysette wouldn't remember, he had hoped that somehow it would connect when she saw him again. When it didn't happen, he hadn't known his reaction would be quite so strong. Lysette just stared transfixed at this man with the over-powering demeanor.

"See, here, mister, whoever you may be," the weasely blonde spoke up, "we'll not have you shout at our friend here, cause a scene, and upset her unnecessarily."

At the sound of the nasally voice that grated on his nerves, Colwyn felt like punching him right out of his seat and ridding himself of this nuisance once and for all.

Susan chose this moment to cut in when she noticed an irritating black frown flash across Colwyn's face and sensed the tension between the two. "Hold it a moment there!" she tried to act as a mediator. "If you'll give me a chance, I'll try to explain. This is Mr. Colwyn Campbell. He claims to be Lisa's fiancé. Although to him, her name is Lysette. Isn't that just the most amazing coincidence?"

"Why this is the most wonderful news!" Lorna finally found her voice and exclaimed as she stood up to shake his hand and draw him into the group. "We're all so very glad to finally meet you. I'm Lorna Tompkins, one of Lis—I mean Lysette's new friends, and this is Stacy, Steve, Rick, and Jerry," she went around the table as she indicated each one.

Colwyn shook each one's hand, but couldn't help hesitating slightly when it came to Jerry. He wasn't really of a mind to be pleasant to these strangers, when all he desperately wanted to do was grab Lysette up and run like hell. Yet he knew that would cause more problems than he was ready to deal with, so he tried to smile politely at each one.

Lysette now found herself quite speechless. She could only sit and stare in shock and confusion at this handsome stranger. It had all happened so fast. It wasn't the way she had envisioned encountering someone who claimed to know her. She had hoped she would remember something once she saw them, but as yet she was still drawing a blank.

"It's been a pleasure meeting all of you," Colwyn tried not to sound rushed and abrupt, but didn't quite accomplish it, "but I'm afraid we must take our leave of you.

Lysette . . ." he urged as he held out his hand for her to grab and assist her up, "you must trust me. I'll explain everything on the way as we have to leave right now for we haven't much time left."

Lysette pulled back from his extended hand thinking, *Who does he think he is, just expecting me to get up and go with him? Doesn't he realize I don't remember him? What is wrong with giving me time to remember or at least get used to him?*

She found her voice and said, "Well, I'm afraid it just isn't that easy. For you are still a stranger to me and I'll not go anywhere with you alone."

Colwyn didn't have the patience to deal with Lysette's resistance just now, although he did see her point. Frustrated and worried he said, "Lysette, we haven't the time to argue just now. We must hurry."

"I've had just about enough of your attitude, fella," Jerry spoke up now in his most hostile tone. "The lady here told you she didn't want to go with you. So leave it alone and back off. Besides, how do we know you are who you claim to be? You haven't shown us any ID and it's obvious she doesn't remember you. For all we know, you could be some loony off the street who decided he'd like to try and exploit her for his own personal gain after seeing one of her flyers displayed around the city."

From the look on Colwyn's face, he was becoming even more outraged at this irritating milksop, if that was remotely possible. He started to solve that problem by leaning forward and drawing back his fist to knock him out with just one punch when Lorna intervened to stop the impending blow by placing her hand on his cocked arm. She calmly said, "He's right about one thing, you know. You haven't shown us any form of identification.

Have you a driver's license or some sort of credit card with your name on it?"

"No, I'm afraid I haven't any of that!" he stated forcefully.

He wondered, *What would she'd think if I told her I have no idea what she is talking about? Whatever happened to taking a man for his word anyhow? Was everyone now so untrusting? If this is the case with the people in this time period, I'm glad I'm not staying.*

Rick then chose to speak up and give his opinion. "Yeah, man, we really need some proof you are who you say you are. We can't just turn her over to you otherwise."

Susan chose to speak up and come to Colwyn's defense. "I believe he's telling the truth. It's just a feeling I get when I look at him. He's already confirmed to me that he doesn't know how to drive and he has no need for a credit card. He even acts as if he doesn't know what it is. I mean, doesn't that prove he very likely comes from the same place as Lisa? I believe they're from a society that shuns the conveniences of the modern-day world. They must live a simple, wholesome life that sounds refreshing."

To Jerry, she made it all sound as if it was some romantic fairy tale come true and that positively turned his stomach. "Sit down and be quiet," he told her, in his most rude and over-bearing manner. "Those are just your hormones working overtime, Susan. You're speaking poppycock and it proves nothing of the sort. Most likely all it proves is that he's an escaped con working on his next score."

"Would you quit being so cynical and negative," Lorna admonished him. "I believe I have a solution to the problem. Mr. Campbell, if you are who you say you are, then surely you won't mind Lysette staying with us just a while longer. That way you can come visit with her every day. If you're really her fiancé, and she truly loves you, she'll eventually remember you and then won't mind resuming where the two of you left off."

"That doesn't happen to be an option in this case," he told her in his most stern voice.

Then he turned back to Lysette and softened his tone to be persuasive saying, "Lysette, please, search your heart. You must remember that I love you. If you'll only try just a little harder I know you'll remember something of me. Try to think back to the night by the pond. That was the most important night of my life. The night I first confessed my love for you."

Lysette drew in her breath from alarm. She had been sitting there open-mouthed, watching these people try and decide the course of her life as if she wasn't even there. She had come so close to just running out and having been done with the whole lot of them. Now this stranger had mentioned a pond and she couldn't help but wonder if it could be the pond she saw every night in her dreams. It was too much of a coincidence and she couldn't think straight because every time she tried to remember, her head started pounding. She wanted so much to believe it was this man's face that appeared in her dreams at night but as yet it had never been revealed to her. What kept running around in her head were two questions: *If he were truly my fiancé, why would he not agree to Lorna's perfectly reasonable suggestion and what was the big rush all about?*

She told him, "I'm sorry. I just don't understand why you can't give me time to remember you?"

Before he could reply to her statement, Lorna offered another possible solution by saying, "If you still insist Lysette must go with you, why don't you give us your address so we can stop by and visit with her each day till she feels at ease with you and actually does remember something?"

"That is definitely not possible," Colwyn told her. "Once Lysette agrees to come with me, I'm afraid you'll never see her again."

Time was running out and he had no patience left to explain any further to these people.

The women gasped in shock at his harsh declaration, but Jerry was plainly outraged. "All right, mister, that cuts it. There's no way we're letting her go anywhere with you. Buster," he called and motioned to the big, burly bouncer, leaning up against the bar, just a few feet away, "would you step over here for a moment?"

Colwyn stood on his guard and watched the huge man glide over. He knew the enemy was calling in reinforcements. As soon as the man arrived, Jerry piped right up and announced, "This gentleman, and I use the term loosely, is disturbing my lady friend here. Would you kindly remove him from the premises immediately?"

"Is this true, ma'am? Is he bothering you?" the giant asked her expectantly.

Lysette found she didn't know how to answer him. Colwyn wasn't actually bothering her but she did feel awkward with him staring down so hard and angry at her.

When the bouncer received no response from her, he decided to ask yet another question. "Well, do you know him?"

He waited for her reply, getting a little annoyed at her silence then she stammered, "I . . . I . . . don't know. I don't remember," she finally admitted, feeling confused and dejected.

"That's good enough for me," Buster stated. "Sir, will

you kindly follow me and leave the lady alone for the rest of the night?"

He tried to urge Colwyn along but he loudly shouted, "No, I cannot! Now, why don't you run along and mind your own business?"

The monster turned ugly at Colwyn's refusal to leave, so he responded by immediately wrapping his huge meaty arms around Colwyn's waist. What he hadn't expected was Colwyn's quick reaction. Colwyn hadn't trained and fought in battle for most of his adult life for nothing and part of his training had been how to fell big giants such as this one. With a quick bend and a jerk, he effortlessly flipped the bouncer over his shoulders, crashing him down hard on the floor.

The commotion they were causing drew the attention of two other bouncers and in a flash they pounced on Colwyn once they discovered their downed friend. Though he definitely had his hands full now, yet Colwyn seemed to still be holding his own against the beefy men.

Lysette felt a churning mass of guilt as she affirmed she was the cause of all this violence and destruction. While she looked on helplessly, she noticed the man was now bleeding from a cut lip and suffering from a bruised eye. She couldn't help but feel sympathetic at the injuries they were causing the man, and she rose to try and put a stop to it.

Jerry had been closely watching Lysette's every reaction since the fight began and when he realized her intention, he rose along side of her, wrapping his arms about her waist and drawing her back down. She tried to throw him off but his arms were like bands of steel.

"It's no use, my dear," he whispered in her ear. "They'll more than likely ignore you. As far advanced as it has already gone, the most you'll accomplish is to end up getting hurt yourself."

By this time Buster had recovered and joined his two buddies in the tackle. It took the combined strength of all three to finally take Colwyn to the ground. After holding him down for a few moments, they grabbed him up and herded him through the crowd toward the back exit. As Buster tossed him out into the alleyway, he uttered a warning remark, "You're lucky I didn't have the police called. If I ever catch you back in here again, you won't get off quite so easily. It'll be the lock-up for you next time, fella."

The crowd had watched, fascinated at this unexpected excitement, but now that it was all over they began to settle back down in their seats. The people around Lysette's table tried to act as if everything was normal, as they didn't want her upset any more than she already was. She kept looking at the exit to the alleyway.

Jerry's hands were still holding her down by the arms and she couldn't rise causing her discomfort and she felt like screaming.

Just then, Susan decided to sit down and join them. Suddenly she found herself in desperate need of a drink and thought, *Maybe it had been a mistake bringing him here. I should have waited until they arrived home; but the man had been so insistent . . .*

Colwyn lay in the dirt for a few moments recovering somewhat before he tried moving. He rolled on the ground next to a brick wall and pulled himself up, brick by brick. Then he dusted himself off and wiped the blood from his split lip. Upon looking around at his dark surroundings, he tried to think what his next move should be. He wasn't going to give up easily as he hadn't traveled through time just to let a few obstructions stop him from getting his heart's desire.

In order to keep his eyes on the front entrance, Colwyn decided to stay hidden nearby and wait for Lysette to leave the premises. Since she wouldn't be in there all night, he planned to somehow steal her away from her friends and then run like hell with her.

Looking around to see if anyone was watching, Colwyn then walked out of the alley and onto the street's sidewalk. He headed toward the parking lot where Susan had parked her car. Upon reaching it, he crouched down and carefully looked around it toward the nightclub. Keeping his eyes on the entrance, it was his urgent desire that she would emerge fairly soon.

While waiting, Colwyn thought over what had transpired inside the nightclub: *Even though Lysette insisted she didn't remember me, I'm sure I saw a flicker of something in her eyes telling me she really wanted to remember. I felt a heartfelt longing from her that reached into my very soul.*

After further thinking things through, Colwyn made a tough decision: *If Lysette doesn't leave this place soon, I will not go back to my own time period without her. We will just live out the remainder of our lives here and try to adjust to a world where we are like fish out of water. One tragic thing though, it would be tragic never to see our beloved families and friends ever again.*

I must say she looked healthy and well taken care of by the strangers with whom she has been staying. I am very grateful for that. Maybe it would not be the worst thing if we have to stay in this time period. I just can't imagine a life without her . . . it is unthinkable. If only she could recall the feelings we shared before this all happened.

While he waited, in his mind he began to formulate a plan to help her to remember.

20

INSIDE THE PADDY WAGON, Lysette was feeling extremely confused and uncertain about the decision she had made in regards to Colwyn. She thought: *When everything seemed to be going wrong, my instincts had cried out for me to put a stop to it and listen to what the incredible stranger had to say. But no, instead I let Jerry coerce me into going against my better judgment. Now I'm really beginning to dislike that guy.*

Some sixth sense made her realize it was important for her to see Colwyn again and speak with him directly. Desperately she hoped he wasn't injured too seriously as the brutes had given him a pretty thorough beating. Not sure why, but there was a conviction inside her that Colwyn was the only one who could shed some light on what had happened to her. In some way there was a connection she felt between them but couldn't explain why or how. She only knew that it felt right.

Lysette was now faced with figuring out how to leave the table for a few minutes to seek him out without causing her friends concern or suspicion. Gazing around the large room she found the answer was simpler than she had first thought.

"Would you please excuse me for a few moments while I go and refresh myself in the ladies room?" she said to the table at large.

"Of course," Lorna answered. "Would you like me to

come with you?" she asked because she sensed Lysette was more upset by what had just happened than she was letting on. Lorna felt Lysette was now in need of a friend with whom she could talk.

"No, no," Lysette insisted a little too quickly. "Everything's all right and I'll be fine. I won't be but a few moments. I promise."

She smiled sweetly at them all before she headed in the direction of the ladies room.

A little too sweetly, Jerry thought, *for her not to have something sneaky up her sleeve. I think I'll keep a close watch on her as she was acting rather strange.*

He kept his eyes on her every step. Just as he had suspected, right after he watched her pop into the lady's room, she popped right back out. She took a quick look around, checking to see if anyone had followed or was paying attention to her. Jerry quickly ducked his head down toward his drink when he saw her glance their way. Out of the corner of his eye he saw that when she was satisfied no one was watching, she turned and quickly headed straight for the back exit from where the bouncers had thrown the man. Right then Jerry decided to follow her but at a discreet distance.

He watched her walk warily down the dark alleyway all the while apparently searching for something or someone! Careful not to make a sound, Jerry sidled up right behind her and decided to make his presence known while she was standing still, apparently indecisive as to what to do next.

"Correct me if I'm wrong," he uttered with an irritating smirk, "but this doesn't appear to be the ladies room to me. Did you happen to take a wrong turn somewhere?"

At the first sound of his voice so near to her ear Lysette jumped. In a split second she turned, faced him and hissed, “Jerry! You startled me. What are you doing out here?”

“I could ask you the same question,” he retorted with a knowing grin. “As I just pointed out, this isn’t the ladies room.”

Though Lysette was quickly becoming fed up with Jerry’s all-too-smug attitude, she realized she would have to come up with an excuse and fast. Thinking fast she said, “Well, of course it’s not the ladies room. I decided I needed a breath of fresh air first as I’m not used to being in a crowded room with that much smoke surrounding me.” *At least that is not a lie,* she told herself.

“Is that what you needed?” he slurred wolfishly. “Personally, I think you need something quite different than that.”

He was standing just inches from her when suddenly his hand snatched out, reminding her of a snake striking, and grabbed the back of her head in a vise-like grip. At the same time, his other arm wrapped around her waist and drew her tightly against him. Greedily he forced her lips to his and thrust his tongue between her teeth. Though she struggled and tried to pull away from him, he was too strong for her. With his mouth plastered over hers, she could barely make a sound. Never, could she recall ever feeling so violated! It was as if he was draining the breath from her body, but still she continued to struggle and resist quite valiantly.

“Quit your struggling, bitch!” he ground out viciously without removing his vile-tasting lips. “You know you want this as much as I do.”

Lysette was able to make a small sound in the back of her throat while he was speaking to her, but she was afraid it was not loud enough for anyone to hear.

Growing tired of her fighting him, Jerry deliberately

grabbed her satin blouse and ripped the neck and sleeve away, partially exposing a soft creamy breast. This inflamed him even more so that he tugged down her bra strap and cruelly pinched the nipple between his thumb and forefinger, causing her to make another sound, this one revealing her pain.

Letting up a little on the force crushing her lips, he then tried to lift up her skirt while drawing her to the ground. The slight release of pressure on her lips was all Lysette needed. Instinctively she came down hard with her front teeth and bit him savagely on the bottom lip. Shocked and in pain, Jerry let out a screeching yelp and instantly dropped her backwards on the hard alley ground.

"You teasing little slut, you'll pay for that!" he angrily promised as he backhanded her hard in the face and threw his body on top of her while his hand smothered her screams for help.

Meanwhile, Colwyn still waited across from the front entrance of the club, never taking his eyes off the door. Suddenly, he heard something that sounded like a skirmish coming from the alleyway from which only minutes before he had emerged. Another person might possibly have not heard a thing, but Colwyn's keen sense of hearing was slightly over-developed from years on the lookout for raiders.

Though he was reluctant to leave his post, he just couldn't help himself. Since it sounded as if someone might be in trouble, he just had to investigate. As he drew nearer to the source, he suddenly stopped short, but only for a split-second. Though momentarily surprised and shocked at what he saw, his reaction time from there on out could be compared to the mongoose attacking its natural enemy, the snake.

In what seemed like the blink of an eye, before Colwyn even had time to think it through, he was standing beside the couple thrashing around on the ground. His movements had been so fast they were almost soundless as he reached down and grabbed the attacker by his collar, yanking him off the woman with just one arm. When he saw that the woman lying hurt on the ground was his own beloved, an uncontrollable rage came over Colwyn and there was just no stopping him. He hit Jerry once, smack dab in the jaw with all his force, knocking him backwards. Instantly there was a loud cracking noise as the jaw broke, causing the young man to lose consciousness. By then Colwyn was beyond reason, having every intention of killing Jerry with his next blow.

When Lysette saw the murderous look on Colwyn's face as he drew back his fist to strike, something inside her snapped. "Colwyn, stop!" she screamed. "Don't kill him! You've already knocked him out. He can't do anymore harm now."

At her plea Colwyn turned, not sure he had heard correctly and asked himself, *Did she actually call me Colwyn or was it just my imagination? Can I believe the sweet sound of her voice?*

Then he saw the recognition there in her eyes. Automatically he held out his arms and she rushed into them. She was sobbing softly and he tried to comfort her with soothing, reassuring words. After a few minutes in the safety of his arms her sobs died down to a lower pitch. When he next spoke she had almost recovered.

"Lysette, I . . . I can't quite believe this is really happening," he uttered as if in a trance.

"Yes, I know, Colwyn," she reassured him. "I remember everything now. It all came flooding back to me the instant I saw that look on your face. I knew you were going to kill him."

"You shouldn't have stopped me, the bastard. If I kill him then he will never hurt anyone else again."

"No, Colwyn!" she pleaded. "I'm sure he'll receive just punishment for his crimes. He isn't worth you getting into trouble."

"You're right," he agreed. "I'm afraid we don't have the time for me deal with him any longer."

Just then, another memory came flooding into Lysette's mind and she said, "Oh, my God, Colwyn, Felicia. . . . It was Felicia who sent me here! How did you ever find me?"

From her tone Colwyn could tell Lysette was quickly becoming very distressed by her memory of Felicia.

"Shush, my love," he soothed as he drew her closer in his embrace. "We'll never have to worry about Felicia again. It's a long story, sweet, and as I said before, we don't have the time to go over it now. I'll explain everything to you once we arrive home . . . that is *if* we have the time to get there. Hopefully it's not too late. Right now, we must hurry back to the First Presbyterian Church because we absolutely *must* be inside it before the stroke of midnight. If not, we'll be stuck in this time period and have to live out the remainder of our lives here."

Just as he finished this shocking revelation, a commotion came from the back exit of the club as a hoard of people emerged from the doorway and headed in their direction. Lysette's group of friends from the table was in the lead. Having become concerned about her and Jerry's failure to return, they had decided to investigate when they heard what sounded like a scuffle coming from the alley. Much to their surprise, several others had also decided to follow suit. So now there was quite a group gathered outside.

Lorna advanced on the embracing couple first and exclaimed, "Sweet Heaven on Earth! What happened here? Lisa, are you all right? We became worried when we couldn't find you in the ladies room. Jerry also disappeared, and then we heard loud noises coming from out here."

"Lorna, calm down. I can explain everything," Lysette told her before Lorna had a chance to say anything else.

When Lorna inched closer to her friend she finally noticed her disheveled appearance and swollen lips. "Oh, my God!" she was quickly becoming excited again. "You've been hurt. Who did this? The police have to be called. You must come with me and I'll take you to the emergency room for treatment. . . ."

She was babbling so fast Lysette had to cut in to get a word in edge wise. "No, Lorna. I can't go with you now. But I'll be fine in a little while, honestly. Right now you must listen to me. Jerry followed me out here then was trying to rape me until Colwyn arrived and put a stop to it."

By now, the rest of the group had noticed Jerry and had begun to gather around him. They were more than just mildly curious as to what had occurred here. Several of the onlookers tried to listen to Lysette's explanation as she talked to the other woman. The words "attempted rape," spread through the crowd like wild fire.

Meanwhile, Lorna became aware of the obvious familiarity between Colwyn and Lysette standing before her. "Colwyn?" she echoed with a puzzled frown.

"Yes, Colwyn!" Lysette confirmed with excitement rising in her voice.

"I remember everything now, Lorna. It all came back to me at the height of the trauma. Colwyn is the man I was going to marry that day I first appeared."

Relieved happiness spread across Lorna's face at this piece of news. "Oh, I'm so glad it finally came back to you but I'm just sorry it had to be under those circumstances."

At that moment, the owner of the Paddy Wagon, after being informed of a disturbance outside, finally came hurrying through the crowd. He hadn't been there earlier when the trouble with Colwyn had come about, but had arrived soon afterwards and the bouncers had made it a point to tell him. When he was informed, he was confident they had dealt with it effectively. Now he must see to this trouble himself.

"Here now!" he shouted over the crowd in order to be heard as he entered the heart of the disturbance. "What is all this trouble about?"

He stopped short when he noticed the unconscious, injured man on the ground. Before he could even ask, Lorna answered his unspoken question saying, "The man on the ground is in that condition because he tried to rape my friend here. That is until her fiancé stopped him cold." She indicated Colwyn and Lysette with her hand as she spoke.

The owner peered a closer look at the couple standing a few feet away from him and recognition came to his eyes from the description his bouncers had given him of the man who had been the cause of the damage tonight.

"Trouble seems to follow wherever you appear, boy!" he grunted aggressively at Colwyn. "You're lucky I don't press charges and have you locked up. But I reckon the lady here is grateful you were able to show up when you did. So under those circumstances, I'm willing to overlook the destruction you caused to my place."

Looking back at Jerry while the two lovers embraced the owner asked Colwyn, "Is he dead?"

"Not yet!" Colwyn replied with regret recognizable in his voice.

"In that case . . . Robert!" he called to his bartender standing at the back door looking through the crowd. "Call an ambulance *and* the police," he emphasized. "Immediately!"

Then turning back toward Colwyn and Lysette the owner stated, "You two will have to stick around and tell your side of the story to the police. They'll want to get your statements. In the meantime, this man will need prompt medical attention, so anyone with hands-on knowledge of first aid, get over here and see to him until the ambulance arrives."

Several people stooped to do as he commanded while he continued to oversee the situation.

Colwyn and Lysette frowned regretfully at this unwelcome and unforeseen delay. Realizing their chance to escape was slowly slipping from within their possibility. Luckily the owner was busy with controlling the crowd and not paying them much heed. Colwyn and Lysette stood watching anxiously, waiting for a miracle that would allow them to make a break for it and leave this all behind.

"Damnit!" Colwyn whispered the expletive in Lysette's ear. "If we wait here to talk to their police, we'll never get to the church in time."

Lysette didn't have a chance to respond, as they were interrupted the next moment by Rick, who had been waiting for an opportunity to speak with Lysette.

"Lisa," he said, using the name with which he was familiar, "I'm so sorry that Jerry did this to you. I feel responsible for your pain, as I am the one who invited him along. Believe me, if I had known he was capable of something like this, he never would have been here."

Lysette knew he spoke the truth from the sincerity and true regret emanating from his voice. "I know, Rick, and I believe you," she smiled at him to convince him everything was all right and she didn't blame him. That eased his remorse. "I know you never would have brought someone along if you had known he intended to cause harm. Don't worry about it any longer. I'll be fine. It's over with now and I forgive you," she told him.

Rick returned her smile thankfully and turned to wrap his arm around Stacy and step back a little. He had a feeling the two young lovers wanted to be alone for now.

Lorna kept a close distance and an observant eye on the two reunited lovers. From the way they kept glancing about she had a strong feeling something more than just this unfortunate incident was bothering them. Stepping closer to where they were milling about nervously she said, "You two look a wee bit antsy. I hope you calm down by the time you talk to the police or they may turn their suspicions towards you."

Lysette suddenly got an idea how to solve their problems as soon as Lorna walked up. "That's just it, Lorna, we can't stay to talk to your police. We must get away from here and fast."

Lorna was clearly shocked at what Lysette said, and quickly burst out, "Oh, but you must stay and tell them everything! If you don't they'll issue an arrest warrant for obstructing justice by withholding evidence. Also, they won't be able to hold Jerry unless you press charges."

Lysette responded in a kind voice, "You must believe me when I tell you I'm very sorry about that, but there's just no other way. If we don't get back where we came from, and soon, it will cause a great deal of unhappiness to a very large number of loved ones. So will you please help us?"

Lorna looked uncertain upon hearing this mysteriously urgent plea.

"I wish I had time to explain further, but it's most imperative that we leave now," Lysette continued trying to persuade Lorna at her obvious hesitation to their request.

Lysette then decided to throw caution to the wind and blurted out the truth before she changed her mind. Somehow, she just knew Lorna would be the one that would understand. She began, "Lorna, we don't belong here. We're from another time and place . . . a time long ago. I know it sounds like I'm crazy, but everything I'm telling you is true. But what is most important is that if we don't get away from here by a certain deadline, we'll never be able to go back home."

Lorna contemplated Lysette's words only for a moment. From somewhere deep inside she knew that these were not the ravings of a lunatic and said, "I always did have the feeling you were out of your element here. It's nice to know my instincts are not out of sorts as much as I thought," she smiled intuitively. Suddenly she burst out, "What would you like me to do?"

"Oh, that's great!" Lysette exclaimed and breathed a sigh of relief upon Lorna's agreement to help.

Colwyn stood back and watched in amazement as his little fireball worked her magic. He made a mental note to never underestimate her or ever take her for granted.

"We'd like you to keep a lookout for when no one is paying attention to us, so we can slip away from here unnoticed," Lysette continued.

"No problem. I believe I can handle that," Lorna agreed.

The sounds of sirens became quite loud as the ambulance and police vied to see which would arrive first in the alleyway. The ambulance got there first and everyone's attention shifted to the medical team that was trying to revive the injured man. Lorna saw this as an opportunity for the escape as it would probably be the only one they'd get that night.

"Okay, this is it. No one is looking, but you must hurry," she whispered her warning as she tried to shoo them from the shadows and around the building, before anyone saw them.

Knowing she would never see her friend again, and even though they were pressed for time, Lysette couldn't resist one last hug. In her ear she whispered, "Lorna, words are not enough to tell you how grateful I am that it was you I first met in this time period. Thank you for everything you have done to help me adjust. I'll never forget you. I promise."

Lorna was a little embarrassed and overcome by Lysette's show of emotion. Close to tears herself, she humbly responded, "Oh, you know, it was no problem. I'm also glad I had the opportunity to get to know you. You're the most extraordinary person I've ever met and I've a feeling my life will never be the same again. But it's a good feeling though," she assured her just in case she thought otherwise.

"Oh, Lysette," she gasped as a thought occurred to her. "You mustn't forget that gorgeous wedding gown of yours!"

Lysette looked up at Colwyn hopefully but he said, "I'm afraid we won't have the time to retrieve it."

"But, Colwyn, it was your mother's!"

Colwyn smiled down reassuringly at this beautiful vision going home with him and said, "Somehow, in this instance, I think she'd understand. I feel strongly she'd approve if you gave it to your lovely friend here."

"I feel that way too," Lysette smiled back at him. Then she turned to Lorna one last time and told her, "You keep it, I want you to have it."

Lorna was stunned at this unexpected act of generosity and tried to refuse saying, "Oh, but I couldn't! It's much too expensive."

"Nonsense. It's my gift to you. That way I'll know you'll never forget me!"

Lysette had to throw these last words back at her friend because Colwyn was dragging her away, around the corner and out of sight.

"As if I ever could," Lorna whispered to herself, as she watched them disappear from her life forever. "I hope you make it to wherever you're going," she tossed the wish to the wind.

Lysette was hard put to keep up with Colwyn's long strides, as they made their way along the street, heading in the direction of the church. Suddenly Colwyn realized Lysette was peculiarly quiet and he incorrectly assumed it was the dress that was bothering her.

"Don't worry. We'll get you another one and it will be even grander this time!"

Lysette looked up perplexed. "What?" she exclaimed, puzzled by his meaning.

"The wedding dress," he explained. "We'll get you another one. Since you were so quiet I just thought. . . ."

"Oh, no, no, I'm not worried about that," she reassured him. "I'm so quiet because I'm thinking how happy I am that you came to get me."

"Could you believe otherwise?" he chuckled with certainty.

"No, not when it comes to you," she chuckled back

teasingly. "At this moment all I can think of is you and home. Right now I don't care if I get married in a grain sack just as long as it's with you."

"Hmm," Colwyn mumbled wolfishly. "That just might make for a charming sight. Don't let me forget to remind you of that idea."

Lysette laughed at his sexual banter and punched him lightly on his upper arm. "Oh . . ." she tried to sound frustrated, but to Colwyn's ears, she didn't quite make it. "There's just no helping you," she declared with finality.

"I certainly hope not."

Colwyn twitched his eyebrow up and down in a suggestive manner. Lysette couldn't wait to get him home.

21

WHEN LYSETTE AND COLWYN FINALLY arrived at the Presbyterian Church, they found all the doors were locked. They tried each one but to no avail.

"What do we do now, Colwyn?" Lysette anxiously asked as he tried the last door. "It doesn't appear we'll be able to get in."

"But we have to get in!" Colwyn told her. "Ian told me it was imperative we return to the place, to the very spot where I first arrived. Otherwise, he said he couldn't bring us back."

"Ian?" Lysette puzzled over the name.

"He's part of the long story I will tell you but it will have to be later."

"Ohh. . . ." Lysette drew out the word while she nodded her understanding.

"It looks as if there is no other choice but for me to break this stained glass window in order to make an opening large enough for me to crawl through. Then I will go around and unlock the door from the inside and let you in," Colwyn said.

"But Colwyn, that's sacrilege to damage church property! I don't feel very good about it," she emphasized.

"I'll just have to ask for forgiveness later in my prayers. I don't see any other way around the problem."

"I guess you're right," she acquiesced.

“Look around the area for something heavy that I can throw through the window,” he told her.

Lysette quickly looked all about her and saw a large, baseball-size rock lodged under a bush. Hurriedly prying it free, she brought it over to Colwyn, who was still standing close to the window. “Will this do?” she asked handing it to him.

“This should accomplish the task quite effectively,” he told her, testing the heaviness in his hand. “Well, here goes,” he said right before he leaned back and heaved the heavy rock through the glass. Lysette didn’t wait but hurried over to wait at the front entrance of the church.

When the window broke it crashed loudly into many stained pieces. The noise was so loud it startled Reverend Morgan who at that very moment was just returning to his office in order to retrieve the notes he had forgotten earlier. Upon hearing the noise, he rushed to find the source of the sound, completely disregarding his own safety. He was taken by surprise and suddenly stopped short at the sight that met his eyes. There was the same young man he had earlier helped about to hurl himself through the broken glass.

“Mr. Campbell!” he bellowed. “What’s going on here?”

“Reverend, we had no idea you would be here. We thought everyone was gone. Upon trying all the doors we found them locked,” Colwyn explained.

“Well, I was on my way home when I realized I’d forgotten my notes from earlier. As I entered my office, I heard the sound of breaking glass,” the reverend explained.

“What do you mean by we?” the reverend questioned as he looked about for this unseen person to whom Mr. Campbell kept referring.

“Why, yes, Lysette and I, my fiancée. Because of your

help, I was able to find her and she has agreed to come back with me. She's standing right outside the front entrance of the church."

The reverend beamed a beautific smile of pleasure at this happy news. Looking beyond Colwyn he observed a beautiful woman standing by the big double oak doors, waiting in the moonlight. "Well here, let me let you in by unlocking the door for you and your lovely fiancée."

"Lysette!" Colwyn called to her. "The reverend is here with me and will unlock the front entrance so we can go in with him."

Lysette smiled her gratefulness as Colwyn neared her. The reverend again spoke, "I'm sorry, I didn't realize you were returning here tonight. If I had known, I would have waited for you or at least showed you where I lived so you could have come to see me there. It is just around the corner."

"I'm sorry also," Colwyn apologized. "I thought I had told you before."

"I must have forgotten," the reverend said.

Colwyn used that excuse to explain his appearance at the church that night.

"Will you forgive my destructive blunder?" Colwyn asked.

The reverend just smiled slightly and stated, "My son, that is what I do. Now, can you tell me why it's so important you get in here tonight that you had to break a window? Whatever it is, couldn't it have waited until morning?"

"I'm afraid not, Reverend," Colwyn assured him. "I'm afraid and almost positive that if I told you the real reason, you wouldn't believe me."

"Oh, I don't know. Try me," the reverend urged. "I've heard just about everything you could imagine."

At that moment a very loud wailing sound could be heard coming down the road towards them. Colwyn listened to the sound with mounting dread for now he recognized it from earlier. "The police!" The words came out in a whisper, yet the reverend heard it.

"Yes, I'm afraid they're on their way here. You see, when you broke the window, a silent alarm went off. They'll want to investigate to find the cause and possibly stop any potential law breakers."

"Reverend?" Colwyn couldn't hide the concern in his voice. It urged for his understanding as he said, "They mustn't find out we're here or all is lost."

"Why?" the reverend asked unusually calm. "Have you done something that could be considered unlawful, besides breaking my window?"

Colwyn decided the truth would be best in this instance and said, "I've hurt a man. It could be serious. At this point, I don't know. All I can tell you is that he was trying to rape Lysette, and when I came upon the scene, I became so enraged that I might've been a little too fierce in putting a stop to the vile creature. I was told they'll want us for questioning, but it's very important that we're here at midnight. I know that seems strange to you but I'm asking you to trust me. Please let us be here. That's all I can tell you now."

Reverend Morgan watched Colwyn's face as he told him the story and his unusual request afterwards. He seemed to consider the man's words for only a moment before he made up his mind.

"Quickly, we must bring you inside! They're almost here. As soon as you're in, you two hide in the fellowship hall and stay put until I come for you. I'll take care of everything with the police." Colwyn let out a sigh of relief at the reverend's belief in him and his agreement to help.

The reverend unlocked the door to the fellowship hall and quickly ushered them inside. Colwyn wrapped his arms around Lysette's waist and led her through the fellowship entrance just as the police pulled up.

As soon as the police came to the front door of the church, the reverend opened up for them. He was so fast they didn't even have a chance to knock. "Hello, officers, I've been expecting you. I know you'll be wanting to find out the reason the silent alarm went off."

"Actually," the young officer in front said, "we've already deduced the reason for that. We noticed the broken window as soon as we got close to the door. Did you see who did it, Reverend?"

The reverend knew he would have a lot of forgiveness to ask for the sins ahead of him that night. He promised the Lord they would have a long talk later. Turning to the officer he replied to the question, "No, sir. I just figured it must've been some mischievous kids who were frightened away when they heard the sirens. I've had no trouble since."

"Just to be on the safe side," the officer assured, "we'll patrol around the area in case there's anyone still hanging around. We'll have to write up a report on it though. If you'd like, you can wait until morning to come down to the station and make a complaint."

"That will be fine, officers. Thank you very much for your consideration."

"Just doing our job, Reverend. In the meantime, may I suggest you go home and get a good night's rest? It's almost midnight."

"Just heading that way now, officers," the reverend assured them.

"Well, good night and take care, Reverend," they

added in parting as they headed down the steps. "We'll see you in the morning."

"Yes, good night to you also and thanks again," the reverend replied as he closed the door on the two young officers.

Then he hurried to find his unexpected guests and assure them that everything was fine. He found them hidden behind a pew.

"You can come out now," he told them. "It's clear. They're gone."

Colwyn and Lysette stood up with a great deal of relief etched on their features. "Thank you, Reverend," Colwyn couldn't help telling him again. "You'll never know what this means to us."

"I think I might have an idea," the reverend uttered knowingly. Then he asked, "Is there anything I can get for the two of you?"

"No, thank you, Reverend." It was Lysette who answered this time. "We'd only like to sit here for awhile and pray, if that is all right with you?"

"That's fine with me. I have a few things I need to do in my office. If you decide there is something you'd like, that's where you'll find me."

Colwyn and Lysette just nodded as he walked down the hall.

"Colwyn, what is it we're supposed to do exactly?" she questioned him now.

"Nothing much really," he answered. "Just stand in the spot where I emerged from and wait until midnight, which is almost here. Lysette, it is very important that you believe in this as much as I do. If not, it could very likely not work."

"Oh, but I do, Colwyn," she hastened to reassure him. "I believe with every bit of my heart."

Colwyn wrapped her close in his embrace as they stood there a few feet away from the altar. He remembered the last time he had stood in front of an altar waiting and was glad that this time she was here with him.

He felt her shiver a little in his arms and knew it couldn't be from cold. Not on such a warm night.

"Are you frightened?" he asked her with concern evident in his voice.

"Just a little," she confessed. "But that's only because I'm not sure what to expect."

Colwyn mistook her statement as meaning she was unsure of a future with him, as his wife, instead of her uneasiness about traveling through time. She couldn't remember what it had felt like. He couldn't believe he was actually going to say this to her because once it was spoken, he highly doubted he would be able to carry it out, if she chose that option.

"Lysette, if you're not sure about marrying me, I'll try to understand and release you from the bond. I know we didn't have much time to get to know one another better before the nuptials were to take place and I know you were upset about not being given a choice in the matter. It's wrong to marry if you're only doing it to please someone else. So if you want to call it off when we get back and go back to your home, I won't try and force you to stay. All I want is for you to be happy. I've come to realize, in my search for you, that your happiness is more important to me than my own." After he said these words he closed his eyes tightly and prayed she would not choose that course for them.

Lysette listened to him with a great deal of emotion surging through her. She was amazed at his unselfish act after everything he must have gone through to come and get her. It made her get all choked up inside. Then, taking a deep breath when she could speak, she joyously declared, "Oh, Colwyn, I love you so very much! I've loved you from the first moment I set eyes on you. It is just that I refused to believe that love at first sight even exists. I didn't want to believe because it would mean that my life would have to change and I thought I was happy with the way it was.

"But then I saw you stepping out of the shadows with your startling green eyes, and my insides went haywire. My whole world, as I knew it, was about to be turned upside down and I resisted the change. You began messing with my oh-so-controlled emotions right from the very first and I became frightened. No one else had ever affected me in that way. That's why I was so hostile to you in the beginning. I was angry that I couldn't deny even to myself that I was head over heels in love with you and I hadn't the foggiest notion what to do about it."

Colwyn grinned the biggest grin of his life as he wrapped her even tighter in the folds of his arms. "I know what you can do about it," he told her confidently. "You can marry me as soon as we get back."

She returned his hug with equal force. "I will!" was her only answer.

"Colwyn," she reflected after a moment of standing there in each other's arms. "There's still the matter of the broken glass. I feel so awful about it lying all over the floor. With us going back to our own time, I know we'll never be able to make restitution and the reverend has been so kind. I wish there was a way to repay him."

Colwyn chuckled a little and shook his head in wonder. "Lysette," he whispered, "the things you think about at a time like this."

Lysette shrugged her shoulders and confessed, "Well, I can't help it. I want to do what's right."

"I know," Colwyn mused. "Actually, I've been thinking about that too. Without the reverend's help, it's very likely I wouldn't have found you in time. I think I've come up with a solution to our little dilemma. As you know, I have a vast amount of land holdings. How about I donate a large section to the church? I'll deed it over to them. That way, I'll make certain they'll always own it. Will that make you feel a little better?" he asked her with a secret smile tugging at the corner of his lip.

"Yes, thank you, much better," she confirmed. Then she said, "Oh, Colwyn, I want nothing more than to be with you, in our time, where we belong. To raise our children and live out a long and happy life together."

"Lysette," he sighed deeply, "you can't imagine how happy you've made me at this moment."

He had to bury his head in the crook of her shoulder because of the deep emotion threatening to overcome him.

"Oh, I don't know," she smiled seductively as she grabbed and held his face between her two soft hands and looked deeply into his eyes. "I have a very good imagination," her eyes echoed a very blatant invitation in their depths.

Colwyn was lost and drowning in the pool of her incredible eyes. He could help himself no longer. Capturing her soft, pliant lips between his, the kiss felt like it was the sweetest victory of all, becoming the kiss to last through time and space. The last bell chimed the midnight hour as the joyous couple slowly faded from sight.

Epilogue

Reverend Morgan emerged from his office a few minutes later. He called out softly, but received no answer. He therefore went in search through the building for his two late visitors, but could find not a trace of them. *Now, where could they have rushed off to so fast?* he wondered. *Young people, they were always in such a hurry nowadays,* he thought with a secret knowledge and a chuckle. He smiled serenely at the spot where he had last seen them standing together before heading to his rectory. He had a strange compulsion to go and look at the painting again, hanging over the fireplace. It was almost as if an unseen force was drawing him forward. It was a portrait of the Eleventh Earl of Camden, the founder of this church, and his lovely wife, the Countess Lysette. Beside them was a cherub-faced boy of about five years of age trying not to look too disappointed (but not quite succeeding) at his restriction to sit still that long. This portrait had been hanging in every church, on this site, since the first one had been erected in 1711.

As he stood there, gazing up at the happy family it presented, he found himself puzzling over why he hadn't shown this to the young couple tonight. Perhaps it was because of the joyous blessing they were to receive, oh—in about a year.